THE GREAT FALL

THE GERMAN LIST

PETER HANDKE

THE GREAT FALL

A STORY

Translated by Krishna Winston

LONDON NEW YORK CALCUTTA

 **GOETHE INSTITUT**

This publication has been supported by a grant from the
Goethe-Intitut India

Seagull Books, 2018

Originally published in German as *Der Grosse Fall. Erzählung*, 2011
© Suhrkamp Verlag Berlin, 2011

First published in English translation by Seagull Books, 2018
English translation © Krishna Winston, 2018

Second printing 2019

ISBN   978 0 8574 2 534 8

British Library Cataloguing-in-Publication Data
A catalogue record for this book is available from the British Library

Typeset by Seagull Books, Calcutta, India
Printed and bound by Hyam Enterprises, Calcutta, India

THE GREAT FALL

The day that ended with the Great Fall began with a morning storm. The man whose story will be told in these pages was awakened by a mighty thunderclap. Presumably the house, and the bed with it, shook, and continued to quiver for a long, eye-opening moment afterward; the eye-opening part did not apply to the person lying there. Startled out of sleep, he kept his eyes shut and waited to see what would happen next.

The rain had not started yet, nor could any wind be heard through the wide-open window. Instead repeated flashes of lightning. The flashes darted through the man's closed eyelids in brief flares, and the dry thunder that followed at shorter and shorter intervals crackled with increased intensity in his ears.

Startled out of sleep: that, too, did not really apply to the man lying there. The storm's sudden onset seemed not to have surprised him at all. He lay still and let the lightning flash through his lids and the thunder roar through his skull as if this were an every-morning occurrence, an everyday occurrence; as if he were used to being awakened in this way, and not merely used to it but entitled to be awakened in this particular way. The lightning and thunder served as a kind of wake-up music, whisking him abruptly yet naturally from sound sleep to a state of mental alertness, and something else as well: a readiness to face the day, to take a stand, to get involved. For now he lay there, stretched out with the tumult all around him, revelling in it.

After the first rumble of thunder, he had almost jumped up to unplug the television set, CD player and so forth. But in that instant he remembered: he was not in his own house, he was lying in someone else's bed. The place where he had slept was foreign, as was the whole country.

This was the first night in a very long time that he had spent away from his own bed, away from his usual surroundings. Before opening his eyes, he had reached out to touch the familiar wall, which was not there. He had reached into empty space. That, too, did not startle him, merely puzzled him, until it dawned on him: I'm away. I left home yesterday. Yes, I didn't wake up in my own bed, but not in an unfamiliar one either.

In earlier times, whenever he woke up on his first day in an unfamiliar place, he would miss his home. Even upon arriving in the evening in a foreign country, while still at the airport, he would gaze with a sorrowful sense of parting at the monitor that displayed the next return flight. But on the morning of this day, which would bring his Great Fall, he was not merely not troubled for even a moment by being in a foreign place but promptly felt at home there. He wanted never to open his eyes again.

It was thunder and lightning, lightning and thunder that now made him feel welcome far from home. And as they gradually died down and ebbed away, the rain took over. Suddenly, in the silence following the thunderstorm, the downpour began, a steady, unceasing clatter. Sheltered by the din, the man lay there, his eyes still closed. Nothing could hurt him. Even if that were the Great Flood out there, he was in an ark, safe and sound.

A third element cradled him as well. He had slept and woken up in the bed of a woman who was fond of him. Who loved him? She had indicated as much at one point in the course of the night. But he would not have agreed to seeing that written down here in so many words. She was fond of him—that much he could say.

He was fond of the woman, too, that morning, more intensely than during the night, or more completely, but in a different sense. She had left the bed and the house very early, before daybreak, to go to work. She had made hardly any noise, and he, lying there half-asleep, had been filled with an almost childlike gratitude, had become the very embodiment of gratitude. He would never, ever, have been able to say this to her, but as he heard the whisper of air in her wake grow fainter as she moved from room to room, he lay there and revered her, that woman.

He would sooner have agreed to being described as her admirer than as her lover. One time, when she addressed him as the latter, proudly, he thought, he had raised his eyebrows and averted his gaze, and not only because he was past the age for acting the lover.

Enveloped in the rain and its steady drumming, which was not accompanied by any wind, he fell asleep again. Although he had various things pending for this day and especially the next, it felt as if he had all the time in the world, and also as if this were already part of, and the beginning of, the confrontation awaiting him. It was such a light sleep that the man floated away in it.

If he still embodied anything, then only sleep. In films, when actors portray people sleeping, no matter how authentic it looks, they almost always fail to be entirely convincing. But this man, despite remaining fully conscious after first waking, actually slept while playing a sleeper, and slept and slept, and played and played. And if he dreamt while sleeping, dreaming something for the benefit of the spectator, it was only that floating again, and floating away. It was a dream without action—for instance, he could not fly. But allegedly the dream-floating, like being able to fly, had a meaning. Except that he had forgotten what it was, as he had forgotten much over the years, intentionally so.

This is the moment to mention that the man whose story is being told here is in fact an actor. In his early years, he had learnt a trade in his father's small business and had often, working beside his father, laid floor tiles in the more-than-modest suburbs to the northwest of B. He still showed signs of this trade, not only on his hands but perhaps even more noticeably in his movements—the way he often took a few steps back, walked backwards, then forwards—and in his searching gaze, especially in his habit of looking up abruptly, after staring for a long time at the ground, of narrowing his eyes in certain film scenes, for no particular reason, completely without ostentation, not intending to convey a conventional meaning, as other film stars had been taught to do. In his case, this behaviour had become—what do they call it?—second nature, or nature itself?

Really—the story of an actor, in a single day, from early morning to late at night? And of an actor not engaged in his usual activity but off the set? A person like that as the hero, more or less, of a story, and a serious one to boot? No one more at risk, no one steadier on his feet than an actor, one like him. No one less of a role-player in real life. He, the actor, as an 'I'! An abundance of absence of ego. Without having to portray characters—in short, not acting—out of commission for days. A person like that lends himself well to a narrative, is grounded. Perhaps a story can be told about him better than about almost anyone else.

He had spent his early years as a stage actor. The theatres were small but his roles were always the big ones, from the beginning. And despite his youth he almost invariably played the ageless heroes: Odysseus; the angel who accompanies and guides Tobias when he sets out to find a cure for his father; Othello, without dark make-up; the baker in *The Baker's Wife* who eventually forgives his adulterous wife and takes her back; Emil Jannings, when he blurts out how 'terribly painful' it is to be 'alive and alone at the same time'. Ageless heroes, or idiots, like Bennie in the stage version of William Faulkner's *The Sound and the Fury*, where the small-town stage expanded to capture the entire universe in the pitiful gaze of the 'house post', as the mentally retarded used to be called; or childlike figures and lifelong children like Parsifal or Kaspar Hauser, in which latter role he reminded a mother, seeing a play for the first and probably last time in her life, of the son she had thrown out of the house, now in his barracks beyond the seven mountains where he was working as an unskilled labourer in construction. On the stage, her son had filled her with such pity that she had promptly set out and brought him home, for a while. The only role the actor had refused to play was Faust, although he was often urged to do so, and to this day he considered that character's ceaseless striving, his ticket to salvation, not even worth a pantomime of spitting.

His films had made him a star, yet, with rare exceptions, people hardly ever recognized him on the street, which remained his element. Everything about him—his figure, his posture, his movements —was inconspicuous, besides which he had the ability to make himself invisible. At least he felt certain he could, and up to now it had worked. In a film, however, not matter which, he was immediately recognizable, who knows why, even in the midst of a crowd or in the very back. It always went beyond simply being recognized and was not a question of the light. Or, rather, it was—though not of the lighting—or perhaps it was, after all. In the very first shot, he stood out, for better or worse, so distinctly that one would not want to run into someone like that on the street, even in broad daylight. Early in his film career, people still compared him to other actors: a darker version of Richard Widmark; a Marcello Mastroianni without the distinctive ethnic features; a Francisco Rabal who had never really been young. Later, it was enough to see him as himself.

It had been a couple of years since he had appeared either on the stage or in a film. Still filled with respect for his profession and, if not proud, at least satisfied with and grateful for the years it had given him, he no longer considered himself an actor. According to him, a person who did not agonize day in, night out, including during periods of leisure, over the problem, the beautiful, constraining, liberating, gratifying and tormenting challenge of portraying lives had no right to call himself an actor, a word that had a different meaning for him than for many others. The word, the name 'actor'—a certain ring.

To no longer act: not his choice. Yet roles had continued to be offered to him as if nothing had happened. And perhaps nothing had. Except that, as he said, the certainty (once again his 'certainty . . . '), from one moment to the next, 'at one blow', that for an actor, and not merely for an actor like him, nothing remained to perform, at least not in a film. There were still parts, plenty of them, and not only the familiar kind, the type-cast ones. But no stories remained to be told, and by story, he said, he meant not the usual kind, 'based on a true story', but a revelation, whether the revelation of a person's face, such as used to happen in the stories filmed by Carl Theodor Dreyer, Robert Bresson, Maurice Pialat, John Ford, Satyajit Ray, or the revelation of an Other, a greater being, of greatness, in you and me, or simply the revelation of someone just being born in a person on his deathbed, of an empty shoe as the symbol of a mute death cry, of a teaspoon falling from someone's hand as the symbol of a greater fall.

He had set out the previous evening, leaving behind his house and his country, not specifically for the sake of the woman here. Rather, he was supposed to start shooting another film after all, the next day, here in this city of hers and its environs, to appear in a filmed story. The story dealt with someone who sets out to run amok, first in his head, but then . . . While reading the script, the actor had felt almost sure of what it called for. If the script could not do it, his acting, his presence, his standing and looking around, would help the story come to life. Now, however, it was no longer so clear to him.

During this back and forth, he had got up. The empty bed. The rain outside the open window. No wind. At a distance from the window, a wavering line of trees on the edge of a forest. In-between, a garden, more a meadow actually, empty except for the summery grass, waist-high, kinked in places by the downpour or flattened. The window was actually a French door, with two wide panels that reached almost to the ceiling. The room belonged to a freestanding house, centuries old. Once a hunting lodge, it was now occupied by the woman. She could afford it; in the nearby capital, she headed a company, which company or of what kind he did not want to know; even the information he had was almost too much.

The fragrance of the chestnut trees' strings of blossoms, wafting in foaming waves from the forest and across the grassy meadow. In the rain-drenched sky above, the circling criss-cross flights of the swallows, so high up that it was as if they were anticipating the return of blue sky and sun. But earlier, too, the swallows had swooped way up high, if possible even higher than now, through the dark cloud banks quivering with lightning bolts, easily giving the lie to the old saying that swallows fly low before a storm.

Naked as he was, he went outside. No one could see him, he had decided—and what did it matter anyway? Where the grass still stood upright, the soaking-wet summery fronds brushed his hips and belly. Bending over, he washed his armpits, face, eyes, ears and hair. The rain continued falling, evenly and strongly. And in fact strength flowed from it. It made one frisky. The rain was warm, and after a few steps cold, then warm again and so forth. He would not need to take a shower back in the house.

A large, dark bird burst out of the depths of the grass and sped like an arrow towards the woods, cawing or cackling, keeping low, its dark plumage abruptly flashing yellow. At one time, the actor had known what this bird was called. But in the meantime, he had forgotten, and that, too, had been the result of a conscious decision that applied to almost all names. Instead, he called after it, as he would seldom have done in the past, 'Hallo, there. Not so fast. I shan't hurt you. Come back and let me tell you something.' And since he was accustomed to listening to his own voice, it struck him that it lacked resonance. The words he addressed to the bird were the first he had spoken on this day. It seemed to him they had not hit the right pitch. And so he spoke the words again, trying them over and over, until, when the yellow-bellied bird had long since vanished, the words addressed to it and his voice had achieved a kind of harmony.

In the kitchen, the radio was on, the sound turned down so low that it created an impression of circling, though different from the circling of the swallows. The world news was being read, over and over, and the almost-inaudible, or perhaps all-the-more audible, announcers' voices seemed to come from the most distant reaches of outer space, beamed to a different universe. 'This is Radio Venus.' 'This is Radio Cassiopeia.'

As he listened, the rushing of the rain broke off, from one moment to the next. But no, the rushing continued, just as loud. Once he registered it, he turned off the radio and pulled, no, ripped out the plug for good measure. He, who usually had a sure touch for everything, reached for the loaf of bread but missed, and again, several times. Not only did he flail around, he could not lay hands on the loaf, no matter what he did. All the strength had drained from his arms, from the right one with which he was trying to get a grip, as well as the left.

The same thing occurred with other objects. The mug he wanted to pull towards him, the spoon in the honey jar, the slice of lemon, the flower in a vase on the kitchen counter, the book lying open next to it—he could not manage to touch them with his fingertips, let alone pick them up. He, a master of gesture—whether folding a map, donning a hat, depressing a door latch, tossing a farewell glance over his shoulder, standing in an open doorway and gazing into the distance, and finally hoisting a rucksack or a saddle onto his shoulder—botched every motion or, rather, every feeble attempt at a motion as he stood there in the unfamiliar kitchen, and when he tried to run his hand through his hair, it got caught in his belt buckle, while his other hand, not so much clenched in his trouser pocket as curled up in a cramp, absolutely refused to be extricated from that confined space, whereupon both his hands ended up interlocked in that same pocket, hopelessly stuck.

The actor eventually succumbed to joyless laughter, the kind described in Ray Chandler's detective stories. At the same time, his brow was beaded with sweat and even the backs of his hands grown moist. As he sank onto the stool that seemed have been placed there to receive him, his head flopped back with as much force as if it were being chopped off, as if he were receiving the kind of blow to the neck that kills instantly. And he had been so proud of his strong, sturdy neck.

Now he could laugh again—as one says of a child—but the weakness that had worked its way into his innermost heart lingered. He was trembling. He, otherwise the epitome of equanimity and groundedness, was tremulous. In his years as a tile-layer, working beside his father, who was always impatient, irritable and intolerant, he had developed a special fondness for the level, both as a tool and as a model for how to behave. The air bubble in the eye of the level, when it hovered there motionless, indicating that something was perfectly straight or plumb, received in his imagination the nickname 'peace bubble', and he found just such tranquillity within himself, or he himself was the tranquillity level—could be one or play one, whatever the situation required. And thus, over the decades, he had incorporated his peace bubble into his acting, into his work, and it had proved its worth every time, as only a tool from one's earliest years can.

How to regain that effect? He waited. He had time, after all (or perhaps not?). He listened. The rain, the rain. Don't let up, rain! Don't stop, rushing sound! Yes, listening, that was it. And he looked— looked around, for which he had to turn his entire head, like an owl, because just now at least his eyes could only stare straight ahead. And when he thought he finally had a good grip on the mug, it slipped out of his fingers and broke. It had been the travel mug which he took everywhere, convinced that the coffee, tea or other beverages tasted good only by virtue of its special form and material. There it lay in pieces, curiously large ones, having fallen from his hand in one final aftershock. At least the trembling had not lasted.

He put the pieces back together with some glue he found without any trouble in the unfamiliar house. Yes, the woman's house was still unfamiliar, although he had been spending nights there for years, unfamiliar in the sense that up to now he had never been in most of the rooms and had not opened cupboards or drawers. Then he cut into the loaf of bread, a whole slice—what a comforting sound—and said out loud to himself, 'No day without sliced bread.' This bread-slicing allowed him to merge with all who had lived before him, embodying them anew. (Also those who would live after him? No certainty there.) The mug bonded immediately and he tossed the tube of glue towards the drawer he had left open —it landed right where he had found it.

And talking to himself again: 'You're still a champion thrower, my friend. Your stage name should be Thrower.'

Music: none. The rain was music enough, especially now that wind had joined in, buffeting the house from all sides. It freshened the air and, together with the pouring rain, beat against the whole house in increasingly loud waves. This wind surged around the walls of the house and surged and surged. And again the man at the kitchen counter talked out loud to himself: 'Ah, the wind, how it whooshes. All around. Around the world. So something remains to be done here after all. To accomplish. Wind like this means something!' A chair that had tipped over out in the grassy area, no matter when or how, was set back on its legs by the wind and then stood and stood. Was such a thing possible? Yes.

The actor made it look as though chewing the bread and swallowing formed part of his preparation for what lay ahead, as if he were collecting himself this way, eating and drinking. But in the middle of this ritual, the kitchen door sprang open—like all the other doors, it was not locked and led directly out to the grassy area—and a man, in the form of a rainman—a snowman would have been nothing by comparison—promptly shouted from where he stood on the threshold, under the gutter: 'You don't even love her. I, on the other hand, love this woman—yes, me. Leave my woman alone. Yes, my woman. In the not-too-distant future, she will be mine. You've spent a thousand nights with her and haven't felt anything remotely like love, not once. Get out, you swindler. Beat it. The woman belongs to me, to me!' And having said this, in an accent that perhaps came mostly from agitation, the rainman closed the door surprisingly gently and was gone. Shortly before he appeared, the other man had felt a kind of early-morning desire for a first human silhouette that would give him a focal point for the rest of the day, a 'form fork' (like a 'tuning fork'). Had the intruder been such a silhouette?

My actor went back to breakfasting in peace, eating bite after bite, drinking sip after sip. It was true: he did not love the woman, and had told her so, in the beginning and once more later, and after that it had presumably become unnecessary. 'I don't love you.' And if she had listened the first time, by the second time definitely not. It was enough that she felt love and spoke of love, and that he did not stop her. 'You're my lover. Since my childhood, you're the first person with whom I can really be me. And no one in this region, no one in this country has had more hours of love together than we have. And every time, we've got the best of them. We've let the world have it. We've taken a nice revenge on these times of ours, supposedly all-powerful, supposedly in complete control. We've triumphed over them and they no longer have any control, are out of the running, and we two, both of us, are the ones who count now. We're the ones who matter.'

And he let her have her say, let her have her way. Nonetheless, he missed it, missed 'love'. Without quotation marks: he missed love. He missed it every day, sometimes less painfully, sometimes as the pain of pains, in one way or the other a day-in, day-out pain. Missing love made him furious, at himself among other things, but ultimately extending far beyond himself. To be precise, what was so infuriating was not missing love but its absence. Missing it would have been a form of love, after all, possibly more complete and holding more promise for the future than a love that was present, tangible, graspable, in the sense that one says to someone who is not there, 'I miss you!' and that was a kind of love. He did not miss love. It remained appallingly absent, and so too on this morning, the morning in question. 'And yet I do miss it,' he said out loud to himself. 'Without it, without being blessed by it and with it and through it for so much as a moment, my day doesn't deserve the name, and I'm just a type who fritters away the day. On the other hand, I'm glad to be rid of phoney friendship once and for all.'

Rain and reading. The actor was a reader. Though the book on the kitchen counter described a sort of running amok, he was not reading it in preparation for his part. He was one of those peo-ple who never prepared, and that was not confined to his profession. With a film role in the offing, he made a point of relaxing, sought distractions, let things take their course, let them happen. In that sense perhaps, he did prepare after all.

At the beginning of the book, the main character had been having breakfast, just as the reader was doing now—which did not worry him: he was reading, and all that mattered was the story which engrossed him. One could imagine the story's hero, sitting there drinking tea with his eyes fixed on a distant horizon, as inspired. On this day, he would undertake something great—paint the definitive picture, capture the long-sought child-murderer, meet the woman of his life, catch someone as he jumped out of a burning house.

As could almost be expected in such stories, the day then took an entirely different course, and all because of a single seed that fell to the ground as the man was squeezing a slice of lemon into his tea. When he bent down to pick up the seed, it was so smooth and slick that it slipped through his fingers, and then time and again. He could easily have waited until the thing dried out. But no: he had to pick up the seed that very minute, it had to be done now, everything depended on it. Except that he could not do it; every time this object, not even the size of a pea yet more slimy and streamlined than a pea, slipped and slid, skidded and skittered away from his fingertips, finally shooting across the room and under the fold-up bed; when he got down on his stomach, with a broom in one hand and a torch in the other, he spied the whitish seed in the farthest corner under the bed, which was too wide for him to reach the spot with the broom, and also impossible to move because it was bolted to the wall; the seed glowed and flashed at him from the darkness, 'a horizon, too, but different from the one far off in the distance that could be seen through the window'.

The chapter ended with the hero regaining his equilibrium after all, going back to his tea at the table and, deep in thought once more, raising the cup abstractedly to his mouth whereupon an ear-splitting crash was heard as the saucer, which had stuck to the bottom of the cup, now let go and crashed onto the table. And again the man might have taken comfort in the fact that the thing had not broken, in spite of the table's stone top. But again no: he promptly grabbed the cup, hurled it against the wall, 'and then not even a miracle could have helped'.

The last paragraph in the chapter consisted of the tirade of insults the hero hurled at the lemon seed, the saucer and many other things: 'Rotten no-goods! Scumbags! Goof-offs! Nazis! Wops! Saboteurs! Alter-globalists! Rootless cosmopolitans! Morons! Vagabonds! Herbalists! Texting fiends! Wheeled suitcases! Stock boys! Passion-killers! False ellipses! Murderous merges! Nasty little men! Sons of bitches . . . '

The following chapter began with the man going into the street. A handwritten note had been stuck in the book there: 'Not to worry—it will end well.' The reader leafed back to the beginning and found the epigraph, an aphorism: 'Impatience is the death of existence.'

As he was used to doing at home, the actor washed the dishes, aired out the kitchen—letting in the rain-laden air, gradually becoming post-rain-laden air—shook out the bedding and did various other quiet chores indoors and out. He puttied one of the old windows that had probably never been tight in its frame from the beginning. With the rain, a swarm of ants had managed to slip inside—a swarm, for these ants had wings. They clustered on both sides of the glass and crept and fluttered around and on top of one another without taking flight. It had been a long time since he had seen ants like this, short bodies beneath long, transparent pairs of wings; he had assumed they were extinct.

On the windowsill stood two glasses from which he and the woman had drunk the night before. After he had washed his, the dirtier one, so to speak, he was about to rinse hers as well. Instead, he left it as it was, gazed at it for a long time, then made a point of pushing it into the light.

He located the vacuum cleaner, vacuumed carefully, including the most hard-to-reach corners, swept the tiled floor in the vestibule, took a wire brush, which he found at once by simply reaching without looking into a cupboard, and used it to scour the sandstone steps at the main entrance, in the process carefully revealing the patterns in the stone, prehistoric spiral-formed shells and jagged traces of ancient oyster shells, polishing them until they shone. Finally, he took a wooden rake and raked the gravel in the courtyard that lay between the house and the grassy area; the torrential rain and the wind had swept concentric rhythmic waves of linden and chestnut blossoms from the edge of the forest towards the house. He dawdled over the raking, almost as if trying to gain time.

Once back in the house, he shaved or, rather, trimmed his beard with the help of a miniature pocket mirror, using the teeny-weeny scissors on his pocketknife. As always, he left for last the two or three distinctly red hairs among all the brown and grey hairs in his beard—they recalled for him his father's evenly reddish beard. And as he now snipped these two or three stubbles, sharper and more bristly than the others, he said, almost without moving his lips and facial muscles, as if he were actually at the barber's: 'Hallo, Father. Here he sits, your son, in a foreign country, sending greetings to you again. I'm still in a good humour here, alone, far from everything, in the house of the woman I consider my co-conspirator. But this evening I'm supposed to be honoured, down there in the megalopolis, before a mega-crowd. And starting tomorrow, I'm scheduled to play a person who runs amok. How am I supposed to survive that, Father? What would you advise? Oh, well, you never gave me advice, fortunately, and I never would have accepted any, at least not from you. Right now your son is still sitting in this quiet house, Father. He's still savouring the day, still savouring life, still savouring being alive, not more, not less.'

Clipping his fingernails: cracked, prone to breaking, as if he were still a tile-layer. Clipping his toenails: the lesions between his toes that had not healed since the days when he stood and worked barefoot in wet concrete, the 'mud', convinced he was unlike everyone else and nothing could hurt him.

Ironing his one good shirt—starting tomorrow, he would be wearing a costume, including when he was not on set—from his travel satchel, so small that he could tuck it into his armpit. It was as if he had been hiding the pouch there and now pulled it out. A linen shirt, white and collarless, still warm from the iron as he put it on. (Where the iron was kept in this unfamiliar house had also come to him with somnambulistic clarity.) Polishing his one pair of shoes with a dab of shoe cream hardly the size of a marble yet sufficient for all the leather, leaving a faint film of black in even the deepest wrinkles. Next, as he did at home, he placed the creamed and buffed shoes in the refrigerator, to be ready when he set out. In his imagination, he was serving as his own aide-de-camp in an old-time regiment.

All these activities my actor had carried out in the parlour, his ear initially still picking up sporadic raindrops as they plopped, who knows how, from the top of the chimney into the fireplace, a sound in the room like an irregular ticking, made by the drops as they hit the logs there and, more audibly, the crumpled paper. Then the ticking had fallen silent and in its place—with no other sound far and wide—the cooing of doves filled the house, coming again from high above but sounding, conducted by the chimney, as if the pair of doves were cooing right by the actor's ear and, as he went about his tasks, he was picturing what it would be like when the evening with the festive crowd was behind him and he would sit at midnight at the table with the woman, asking her factual questions, not for the first time and with her cheerful assent, about the physical sensations she experienced when making love, and she would describe them to him just as factually, and describe and describe, on and on, everything she experienced as a woman.

They would sit there with the window open to the night. The table would be the one over there on a raised platform, so they would look like a couple onstage. Their hands would rest on the tabletop with some space between them, quietly, almost without moving, from the beginning of their conversation to the end. From time to time, an owl would be heard hooting from the forest, the only sound coming from outdoors, swinging towards them in the room like a rope, at first just one note, then two syncopated notes and, as the dialogue drew to a close, three such notes.

And this was how the man would begin his interrogation of the woman: asking whether some morning she had woken up with a man inside her without remembering when he had entered her or knowing who this man could be who was inside her, on top of her, beneath her, in a jumble of spatial sensations—as if they were lying indoors and at the same time out in the open, and vice versa—and with the only sense of time being that of morning, even if it was not morning at all, and they had both lain perfectly still, without the slightest movement, she wide awake, the man in a deep yet not deathlike sleep, which would remind him, the interrogator, of a dialogue in a film when Glenn Ford—objecting he is so tired and she is drunk—wants to pull away from Rita Hayworth, whereupon she replies that a drunken woman and a tired man make an excellent pair, in which connection he, the actor, would pre-emptively exclude any possibility of drunkenness on her part: whether, in short, she had ever experienced being together in such a situation with a complete stranger. And she, the interrogatee, would first laugh and repeat 'in short' and then remark that his question had an epic breadth to it and therefore her answer would have to have similar breadth, and would that result in a drama? And at that moment, from the forest, the hoot of the owl, or whatever it was, would make itself heard on the set for the second time.

Clearly, the actor was in no great hurry to leave the property and the grassy area round about. He apparently did not mind that a shoelace broke as he was tying it, and it seemed intentional that when he was tying his necktie, he kept getting the knot wrong. Without having to hunt for it, he found, in a drawer he had not previously opened, another tie, in garish colours that did not go with his shirt and suit at all. And that very fact got him moving, as did the discovery that he had mistakenly put on socks of two different colours and lengths. After plopping a too-big, rustic hat with a moth-eaten brim on his head and sticking a falcon's feather in it, he was ready at last to set out. Pausing on the threshold, he turned back and eliminated all traces of himself. Nothing in the house would serve as a reminder of him and his presence there.

TWO

Upon reaching the edge of the forest, he turned once more towards the estate and felt a certain satisfaction at the thought that the house and grounds did not belong to him. At one time, he had been a property-owner, and enthusiastically so. But by now, owning property had come to seem like a burden. It hemmed him in, constraining him and his perspective. It was as if as a property-owner, he less and less often saw anything whole, overarching, grand, focusing instead more and more on individual details, increasingly only petty ones, and if not that, every aspect of those details that was messy, defective, broken. As a property-owner, one ceased after a while to see the big picture, let alone gaze calmly at it—the details forced themselves upon one and there could hardly be any question of a context when one was monopolized by one's property. Sometimes all that saved one was the sight of something one did not own, especially the sky overhead. 'Hallo, there, property-owner, with your head pathetically bowed over your little patch of ground: Hold your head high and lift up your heart!'

In these foreign parts, the sky was not the only thing that did not belong to one and, in glancing over his shoulder, the man now took in the rusty TV antenna, the rotten spot on a balustrade, the crack in the courtyard lantern's glass shade, the waterlogged old mattress in the nearby shed—saw it all and looked past it. Above the roof hovered a speck of blue that had just sailed to that location.

The forest separated the woman's land from the next settled area and the place where she worked, the capital city. No road led there from the savannah-like grassy stretch. He could have bypassed the forest in her second car, which she had left invitingly in the driveway, with the keys in it. Maybe next time, but not today—that was out of the question for this particular day. 'If there is a next time,' he found himself saying. What did he mean by that? Nothing, nothing at all. He had had nothing in mind. Nonetheless, the sentence stuck with him, bored its way into his brain, and he did not rid himself of it until he had plunged into the forest and walked some distance. And he vowed to stop talking to himself in this frivolous way. But how? Forbidding himself to do it? For a prohibition like this to stick, didn't it need to come from someone other than oneself, some outsider, a third person? 'Hush! Enough! Not another word!'

He had entered the forest through the thicket of wild blackberries that grew along the edge. You should all have seen the way the actor, in the expensive suit the woman had bought him specifically for that evening's ceremony, without a moment's hesitation raised first his left knee, then his right, and trampled the brambles, clearing a path while plucking the first ripe berries and stuffing them into his mouth. One of the berries left a dark black stain on the, 'his', freshly ironed quince-blossom-white shirt—no white more perfect—and one of the thorns, whose local name, *ronce*, had more of a ring to it, snagged the jacket lining. Far from being upset, he actually welcomed these mishaps. Similarly, when he had lines to learn for a film, he would often leave the script outdoors overnight, where the dew would create ridges in the pages, rain would soak it or snow would cover it, as if that were the only way to break the book in and make it his own.

As he headed into the forest, he did not encounter anyone for a long time, which was surprising with the metropolis so close, and he enjoyed this absence of people. He did not mind hearing the roar of expressways in the distance and the sounds of not a few small planes and helicopters almost overhead. Once, he caught an unexpected glimpse through the trees of the skyscrapers that ringed the city, seemingly far beyond the forest and way below. Another time, someone dressed in blue was standing next to a bush; he was relieved to discover that it was a sign, as were the yellow figures he encountered next—markers for gas pipelines.

The forest consisted almost entirely of deciduous trees, well spaced, so walking was easy despite the absence of paths. Yet it was also surprising that after the morning's downpour, the ground was almost dry, at least sandy and not muddy in the least; his feet, damp from the grassy area, soon dried.

Pathlessness and the homeless. They had pitched their tents deep in the underbrush and behind fallen tree trunks and, since his last time crossing through the forest, they seemed to have multiplied. He gave each encampment a wide berth, until he noticed that all the tents were deserted. Now he was no longer encroaching, as someone out in the woods in a suit and tie, on the realm—if indeed it was such—of those who had removed themselves unnoticed, never to return, from the human world, the settled world, the 'ecumene', becoming unhoused and homeless once and for all. So now and then he made a little detour to examine one of the tents, or what was left of it.

Had the former occupants moved on for the summer? At any rate, not one of them would ever find his way back to his camping place here. Each campsite had been abandoned long ago, over and done with, along with the debris left behind—a charred armchair, scraps of newspaper from the previous year and years before, the empty frame of a shaving mirror. Another surprise was to see, quite frequently in the sand and the ashes, oyster shells, also the shells of vineyard snails, labels from not-inexpensive cheeses, smashed wine bottles bearing the labels of notable vineyards and vintages, and not all the brandies had been the usual rotgut. He even found, buried in a damp pile of ashes, a porcelain bowl, slightly chipped along the rim but otherwise unharmed, in Sèvres blue, and he picked it up as if that were perfectly natural, making it his own.

At one of these sites he lingered somewhat longer. A young fellow, an adolescent, had had his lair here in the underbrush. That became obvious from the remnants of a workbook, which, as its subject matter revealed, belonged, had belonged, to an apprentice, a carpenter's apprentice. His name had long since faded, but some descriptions of different types of wood and how they were used in building remained legible. The date of birth following or below his name was still legible; the boy, if he was still alive, was now sixteen, the age of his own son, the actor realized as he crouched by the deserted refuge, the son he had not seen since the boy's childhood.

The young man's handwriting was harmonious and firm; he had apparently taken pleasure in learning his trade. The surviving work drawings, too, expressed a quiet enthusiasm, and a veritable tenderness manifested itself in the pencil strokes with which he had rendered the shading and patterning of wood grains, the different forms of joinery, especially for weight-bearing applications; these strokes had nothing mechanical about them.

It was striking that this youth had taken refuge in, or fled to, a forested area where he was surrounded only by trees to whose wood he was drawn, as the workbook revealed. Not a trace far and wide of the beech, ash or birch trees that did not appeal to him, aside from the fact that such wood was of little use for his trade. Instead, exclusively oaks, with hazels in-between, the latter only as underbrush, each clump, however, forming a circular palisade of equally straight shoots, growing densely upward while bending away from one another like the splints of a basket, and each clump becoming a natural hut if one cut away the shoots in the middle. He had avoided the other types of trees because these provided neither concealment nor protection. Beeches and their trunks always stood there naked and overly visible, without any underbrush around them, for the fallen beechnut shells built up in a layer as deep as one's soles and hard, spiky and impervious to air, in which hardly anything could take root; and birch and ash trees likewise stood by themselves with nothing growing at their feet except perhaps ferns, often nice, thick, tall ones that offered a place where one could lie down for a bit, but no roof, not even temporarily.

The youth had never returned home. He had gone missing, had already been missing the moment he forced his way into the middle of the hazel palisade, with only his apprentice's pouch, of whose contents all that remained were some waterlogged pages from the workbook, and had let himself fall to the ground. He had fallen, never to rise again. He had been loved by his mother or someone, and how! but even love, even being loved, even still being loved, and how! would no longer help him get back on his feet. He had died, not to these or those other people, but to himself, whether dead or alive. He was abandoned, abandoned by himself as by the world. And those of his kind—but no, he no longer resembled anyone, and no one of his kind resembled him or anyone else— were falling by the dozen onto the unfamiliar, and daily more unfamiliar, earth from which they, like him, would never again rise, and most of them little more than youths, yes, children. At this very moment, another child, and then another and another, from one terrifying instant to the next, was falling out of its child's paradise of play, and never again would these children find their way back to their familiar orbit. Game over. Help! But how? Could they be helped at all? Who could be helped any more?

One could not tell by looking at him but my actor had always felt impelled to help, every single day. He thought, or he knew, that help was needed, here, there, more and more. For now, however, all he could do was take the apprentice's workbook with him, which made his jacket pockets bulge even more. No problem—by that evening, they would be bulging unmistakably. (In his films, he often had bulging pockets.)

The sky had suddenly turned blue. It was not merely blue, it was bluing, and bluing. This bluing had the kind of delicacy that made one feel cradled in the certainty that this delicacy would never fade. The whole forest below glowed from the blue on high. And at the same time, as the actor resumed his walking, he saw the illumination of the objects all around as the light of a last day, 'my last day', and again forbade himself to talk to himself this way: 'How irresponsibly you babble these things. You mustn't think such thoughts. You mustn't. It's time to be among people again.'

Then he heard a sound behind him. A branch cracked under someone's feet. But before he turned to look, he realized: the noise came from him. And that did not remain his only self-deception. A helicopter rattled overhead, coming closer and closer: his own shirt flapping in the breeze his walking generated. A crackling in the thicket: from the feather in his hat. A tree creaking as it fell: his yawning. The growling of an invisible dog up ahead: his stomach. A group of walkers who struck up a chorus in the distance: without noticing, he himself, all alone, had begun to sing, to hum. From amid the ferns and tall grasses someone sprayed something in his face: again he was the one, having unconsciously grabbed a particularly swollen jewelweed seedpod in passing.

The bursting of jewelweed if one barely brushed against it: a temporal threshold in the year, in the summer, as the hazel catkins, which had just opened, drifting in the otherwise imperceptible breeze, marked a temporal threshold in early spring, and the gentle crunching of nut shells marked a temporal threshold in early autumn. Once he had been aware of innumerable such temporal thresholds in the year. But meanwhile he had forgotten them all. He no longer knew them, or did not want to know them; for him, they had lost their meaning. There remained only one temporal threshold he could not and did not want to forget: the circling of an eagle, high up and higher still in the sky, calm spirals in the blue, drifting away and finally returning and circling again, while down on the ground, after hours of silence, the hour for an even deeper silence, a palpable one, came due, in which not even a grasshopper's chirping would be heard, only the silence, with its sign, the eagle high overhead, the temporal threshold of midsummer. And as he thought of it, he looked up and there it was, high in the blue, no sooner thought than done, I kid you not, the eagle circling, its motionless wings spread, far above all the fluttering, flapping crowds of birds zigzagging and darting through the air. So that meant today was midsummer.

And yes, there was another temporal threshold in summer that he did not want to forget: the feathers that falcons dropped, God knows why, during a one- or two-week period, never more than one apiece, with brown-green-grey-white tiger stripes, a rarity among the feathers found on the ground in the woods and sometimes also in the street, and now and then a tiger pattern like that even turned up on a square in the middle of Paris, or Rome, on the Plaza Mayor in Madrid. At the thought of the feather, there it would be in front of him, on a pillow of moss, as if being presented to him? No, something even more unbelievable happened: it, the falcon's feather, wafted down, as if just dropped, before his very eyes, swayed and bounced back and forth in the air, up and down, and only when it had almost reached the ground did it fall straight down, quill first.

This was not the first time that something that had just come to mind appeared before him at almost the very moment, and there had been a time when that had not particularly surprised him. He viewed this phenomenon as natural, a law of nature. On this day, however, the phenomenon occurred several times in a row and, although he stuck the feather next to the first one as if it held no significance, it seemed too much part of a pattern. Did fear befall him? Yes, fear of himself.

Please, no signs and portents, no ominous ones, but also no good ones. 'Onwards. Keep going.' Unlike most others in his profession, he did not engage in any sports. Walking was not a sport, at least not for him. And yet he sometimes pictured his walking as a sport, and one he had invented. He had a name for it, too, the 'obstacle walk', 'obstacle-walking', which in actuality was a variation on the steeplechase. He had no use for running, however, except when necessary or in an emergency. 'Running? Life's too short!' Whenever he encountered runners, he made a point of slowing down.

His obstacle-walking consisted, like the steeplechase, of letting obstacles determine his course. If he came upon a fallen tree trunk, a boulder, a ditch, a fence or other such barriers, he did not make a detour around them but tried to go over them. The rule he set for himself was that he must not alter his rhythm. Jumping or climbing was allowed, so long as it fit seamlessly into his regular movement and formed part of his walking. So no pausing or backing up to get a running start, and when climbing, he was not allowed to use his hands. But what kind of climbing was it in which one had only one's toes with which to grip? And quite a few obstacles did not qualify for his sport. On the other hand, he practised it only when he could see the obstacles clearly and assumed they were suitable for the course. And besides, he took up his obstacle-walking only sporadically, when a certain weariness overcame him while he was walking and prevented him from having any other sensation, and afterward he would continue on his way feeling considerably refreshed and—or did he merely imagine this—with renewed resilience. 'The main thing is, I imagine it's effective.'

This was one of the inventions with which the actor played, largely for himself. A different one occurred to him after his obstacle walk, as he quietly resumed his passage through the forest. As he thought about all the nature trails with signs and labels at every turn, providing information not only about trees and plants but also about types of soil and geology, rock formations and so forth, the idea came to him of a 'misinformation trail'. And it would work more or less like this: at every turn, things would be laid out, impossible to miss, which looked so much like other things that at first one could not help mistaking them for those things. And the things they resembled, unlike the ones actually laid out, would all represent something valuable. A swarm of intensely yellow leaves, for instance, would be spread out and fastened to a special pillow of moss in such a way that a person walking along the trail would see in them a carpet, a rich one, of chanterelles/setas de San Juan, and would automatically bend down to pick them. A lump of mica, sticking up out of black or red earth, impossible to miss, would mimic a vein of silver. A piece of birch bark, rolled up and with horizontal striations, would be the spitting image of a medieval scroll. A square of chestnut-blossom strings, seemingly knotted together, would appear to be an Oriental carpet. A clump of wild boar's dung—a black truffle. An oval formed out of beechnut shells would be a cloak of rare shells from the South Seas or wherever. A heap of muted white limestone would be polished to resemble a precious hoard of ivory. An empty wasps' or hornets' nest, rolling back and forth in the wind among fallen brush would be another lost treasure, as a glistening snakeskin, likewise whipping in the wind as it dangled from a branch, would be a valuable object, and a gold-coloured dead insect an Egyptian gold scarab, and a bleached insect's carapace a miniature sculpture of the Buddha in the lotus position.

And the point of such an educational trail? Observation, very close observation, of error, or things erroneously taken for something worth finding, of the source of error, of the object of error, once the delusion became clear. And what did such observation of error reveal? Weren't the erroneous objects—the birch bark, the glittering mica, the hornets' nest, mouse-grey and ragged—worthless upon closer inspection? Actually not—they did represent value. The flash that accompanied recognition of the error would sharpen the powers of observation and the erroneous objects would be elevated to objects of study. They would become novelties, unfamiliar things, previously not viewed in this way. Why 'in this way'? In the retroactive flash stemming from error, an aura would form around the objects, in whose midst the beechnuts, the gold-coloured insect, the wild-boar dung would be sharply illuminated, under a special microscope. And? What then? What to do with the discovery? What value could one attach to a faded insect husk isolated from its surroundings and brightly lit? How much? How many yen or rupees? Let's have the market value, please! The object of error per se: worthless. The value of observing it: priceless. It would all hinge on observation, the ability to observe, on the conversion from idle looking to attentive observation, and, as a result, actually learning or, in other words, taking in something for the first time, thanks to error, and the forms and colours becoming apparent, the intense yellow of the leaves, the structure of the chestnut blossoms, the pattern that emerged in the foam trapped in a hollow between an oak tree's roots; taking in all these priceless riches for the first time and for good—'Otherwise it would not be my nature trail, would it?'

It is easy to see that as a child, long ago, you were already playing with the idea of becoming an inventor. And even then you did not have anything practical and obvious in mind, right? What would your father have said about your nature trail, this trail of errors?

In those days, he would have raised his eyebrows. Today as well, only in another way ... And besides, a trail like that would do more than teach people to recognize and learn about objects in nature, or the colours and forms in a forest: what takes place between you and nature also applies to your life in the world. Your seeking, finding, losing, going in circles, mistaking phenomena in nature and through nature has symbolic value. Processes in nature are symbolic.

Don't you have a word other than 'symbol'?

Yes: example. Nature offers examples. The trail of errors in the forest, the false appearances in nature would constitute examples, unmistakably.

Lost in such reflections as he continued on his way through the forest, perhaps also going in a circle, the actor unexpectedly found himself facing a tree stump as tall as a man. And equally unexpectedly a shudder went through this stump. The trunk whipped around and displayed the face of a human being, a man, an elderly one. Although the actor had approached gradually, his footsteps steady and audible from a distance as he proceeded over the hummocky forest floor, he had obviously startled the old man. Intent on staying away from other human beings as long as possible, the actor had bumped into someone apparently several degrees more in need of solitude. As if to apologize, the actor promptly made a wide arc around the lone figure standing there and plunged into the next thicket. For no more than a second he had the other person's face in his sights before the man turned away and resumed his previous position. But a second could be long. And this particular second was a drawn-out one in which various things were transmitted to the actor, in a quiet, powerful wave. Without imitating him, the actor was transformed into the other man, with a shudder that recapitulated the man's shudder of alarm.

The old man was a migrant, from a country to the east. And he was in the trackless forest as a mourner; had come there to mourn. His wife had died, not just recently but a long time ago, and not here but in the country that had once been their home. And the fact that the man was facing a pair of very young birch trees that he might have planted himself meant that he was also celebrating Pentecost all by himself, according to the custom of his country, or celebrating it belatedly. He and his wife had met as children and had promised themselves to each other. Neither he nor she had ever been with anyone else or, as the expression had it in their country, 'gone' with anyone else. They had remained childless, there was no question of having children and, indeed, no one would ever have asked them about that. The young birches, they, too, a couple, before which the old man was standing, and had been standing for two hours, if not since the previous night; in the other country, they would have been cut down—fetched from a nearby forest—and would have flanked the entrance to their little one-storey peasant cottage. There the birches would have begun to wilt, perhaps as soon as the Monday after Pentecost, but here they remained green and would continue greening and greening, and the feast of Pentecost could be celebrated by the widower into late October. Was he praying? Could one describe his silent vigil as praying? One could. The birch foliage had flickered, a flickering intensified by the raindrops clinging to the tips of the leaves, in which the actor had noticed the sun for the first time on this day, in its reflection, although it had been high in the summery sky for quite a while. The sleeves and trouser legs of the old man's suit were frayed, and an enormous growth disfigured his neck. A cane was leaning against one of the birches, the briefcase at his feet was missing its clasp and one of his shoes its sole, his jacket had lost all but one of its buttons, and that one was hanging by a thread, and his cowlick was caked with dandruff.

'The last human being,' the actor said to himself, 'one way or other. Is this supposed to mean that we humans are done for, I and the others, the world of human beings? Is that possible? Is that permissible? Can it be true? No, it mustn't be true, mustn't be true.' And then: 'Watch what you're blabbering about, even if only to yourself. Blabbering is not merely blabbering, saying is not merely saying; words, even those that go unspoken, are not merely words. Hush, my friend!'

Soon he emerged from the wooded area into the open, not into one of the suburbs of the metropolis but into a clearing that created the impression that only now had he truly made his way into the forest, to its very centre. If the grass around the woman's property had been waist-high, now it was up to his chest. The light had the quality one finds only in a clearing, and a bracing breeze was blowing in which down from dried-up blossoms of the thistles that formed little islands in the grass slowly and steadily drifted through the air above the clearing. No eagle in the sky here, no falcon speeding by with a screech, nothing but the monotonous chirping of the summer crickets filling the entire clearing from deep down in the grass, deep down in—what was it called?—the soil. It made one's heart swell as wide as it could. And the woman came to mind. True: he probably did not love her. But with her he saw himself as enhanced. Was that nothing? He had time. He still had time; nothing more worthy of a human being. 'Hallo there, clouds!'

The large clearing, too, was free of humans, which there, so close to civilization, was all the more palpable—and the longer the condition persisted, the more astonishing. Yet one was not out of the world. Other people existed—but woe unto them if they had the audacity to appear!

Damn! Here they came, first one, then another, then several at a time, then a whole gaggle of them, in the flesh. As with the earlier image of an eagle in the summery sky and the falcon's feather falling in a spiral from above, it was as if merely thinking about one's fellow human beings had called them to the scene. Except that what had seemed in the earlier cases the fulfilment of a wish—let them appear!—in this case was a muddle, devoid of images, which resulted in the exact opposite, as did the subsequent 'Beat it!' that caused their numbers to increase more and more.

The breeze that had rustled so gently through the chest-high grass only moments before now hissed. The blades scratched his armpits and stung like nettles. The crickets' chirping continued to reverberate from all the horizons but it sounded like countless teeth being gnashed in rage. He tried to avert his gaze from those occupying the—his—clearing, staring instead at his fingernails. The nails seemed to grow before his very eyes, developing sharp points, while the hairs on the back of his hands became longer and longer, forming curls and, without any doing on his part, trapping small insects, which got tangled up in them and promptly perished.

Averting his eyes from his hands and nails. Looking up at the sky or in some other direction? No, only back at the people who were gradually filling the entire clearing, from one end to the other. He could not take his eyes off them, no matter how fervently he wished to. For the sight they presented was not beautiful. Or at least so it seemed to him. And in contrast to the occasional professional actor, male or female, he wanted nothing to do with an outright absence of beauty. Not that he aspired to make a point of portraying or evoking the beautiful. But never, ever that which was unbeautiful (which did not necessarily coincide, for instance, with something beautifully ugly): that offered him nothing to portray and evoke. And perhaps he was attracted only to the beautiful after all?

The unbeautiful, on the other hand, he found oppressive. Because it was impossible to avoid—no way to avert one's eyes and shut one's ears to it—it penned one in, narrowed one, twisted one, hurt one, offended one, and one became unbeautiful oneself, a part of the unbeautiful, an outgrowth of it, especially by being compelled to mimic it. Neither in his profession nor outside of it had the actor ever been tempted by mimicry. He despised mimicry and mimics. Even as a schoolboy, he had had a low opinion of the success garnered by the champion mimic—there was one in every class—and when he was the only classmate who could not laugh at the performance, he, he of all people, was dubbed a spoilsport. To him, mimicry was no art, and he believed in art, even if he could not exactly say what that was, at least not off the cuff. Mimicking or aping certainly did not qualify. Yet, occasionally, he caught himself mimicking something; it happened only outside of his profession, and each time it brought him grief and, so it seemed, shame. It simply came over him, which is to say, his mimicking was not something he did intentionally. And he did it badly; ten times worse as an actor, speaker and observer—to whom seeing and observing meant everything. Mimicry just popped out of him, unbeautiful, ape-like. And it did nothing to assuage his shame that he was usually the only one to see or hear it. The compulsive mimicking of the unbeautiful that came over him was supposed to save him from it, and instead he became evil, the evil one, himself. No one other than he had witnessed the phenomenon up to now, except one time, when his son was present, barely old enough to speak. 'Don't, Father,' the boy burst out, 'no!' Or did he only imagine, as he thought now of the sudden fear, almost disgust, in the child's eyes, that his son had said this?

What was unbeautiful about the people who began to usurp the clearing, as if on cue? When he asked himself this question later on that summer day, he no longer had an answer. The repulsion had been instantaneous. Because there were so many of them? At times he felt at home in a crowd (not only, for example, in the theatre or at parties, and certainly not, as would be the case that evening, when he himself was supposed to be the centre of attention). The first glance proved decisive—not something specifically repulsive about the people swarming over the clearing, until then so blissfully devoid of human beings—but the repulsive element, the offensively unbeautiful element, was an irrefutable fact that did not need to assume any specific form.

At second or third glance and so forth, the details emerged, as if perfectly natural, in the shape of various indicators and, upon subsequent reflection, he realized he might have generated them himself, causing the people advancing here, there and everywhere from among the trees into the clearing's wheat-stalk-high grass to appear as an eruption. Whatever the case, the fact that they appeared was simply not acceptable and the way they moved was not beautiful. Not one of them, not a single one, would have come up with the idea, yes, the idea, of pausing for so much as a fraction of a second on the threshold between the forest and the large, open clearing. Without exception, these miserable wretches moved from one area into the other as if there were no such thing as a transition. A deer would have hesitated, as would a hare, unless it were being hunted. Even a hornet flying in a direct line would have circled at the edge of the clearing and a mole, blind though it allegedly was, would have sensed underground the particular light of the clearing, letting it sink in before it went back to burrowing.

These two-legged creatures, on the other hand: neither a 'What's this?' nor a 'Who's there? nor a 'Look!' Occasionally, one of them would pause to snap a picture with his mobile telephone. But actually stopping was something else again. And if one of them had a hand to his ear as he marched by, which merely indicated that he was adjusting the volume on his headphones—it was out of the question that a single person in this motley crew would have cupped his hand behind his ear to listen more intently.

The repulsive thing was that with the best will in the world—no, that would be a lie, for at the first glimpse of them any good will had been down the drain—he could see in the occupiers of the clearing only typical features. They appeared exclusively as types: walkers, runners, bicyclists, elder-hiker-group members, all-ages-hiking-group members, and not merely because he was seeing them from a considerable distance. Types: they were indistinguishable from what they were doing and representing, and unabashedly so. As a result of the initial ill will, but also without it, no traits could be perceived in them other than what was frankly and impudently typical. These figures were loud, loud already among the trees and becoming even louder in the clearing, without being loudmouths. Impenetrable and excessively loud—nothing more communicated itself to the reluctant observer, and the only thing that helped was aping them. Did it help? It did not.

Jogging along was the black TV announcer, who also made documentaries about religious sects, droughts and avalanche barriers, and next to him his new girlfriend, the blond meteorologist. Pedalling by and sending thistledown flying in all directions were the Fabulous Five of plastic surgery. Carving furrows through the wildly waving grass on their custom-designed motorbikes, with only their helmeted heads visible, were the four traders from the Town and Country Bank, presenting themselves as the new Rolling Stones but also a more up-to-date foursome. Striding by with indefatigable vigour, their cross-country ski poles striking the ground with a metallic clang, were the white- and grey-haired superfluous ones. And there—did you see that?—in a sleeveless black track suit, the president of the entire country crossing the clearing on the diagonal, accompanied not only by his security detail but also by the entire Cabinet, to whom he, who, according to his autobiography, had been determined even as a little boy to be active, active, nothing but active ('action is everything!'), looked back over his shoulder as he ran, calling out the actions he had planned for the day and beyond. So there they were, crissing and crossing, the types populating the new world stage? Which of these characters might he have liked to play? Play? Perform? Be? Oh, topsy-turvy world. Oh, time out of joint. And for a moment he saw himself running up to the powerful one and plunging a knife into his belly.

He, a mimic in spite of himself, a jumping jack whose head, neck, arms and legs jerked back and forth as if on strings as he unwillingly observed the scene, did not remain silent. Willy-nilly he had to raise his voice and ape these people whom he would never dream of performing. And if his jerking looked unattractive, my actor's voice sounded as ugly as sin (that same voice which could be so distinctive that it was nearly impossible to dub his films). He pictured, next to him, the reluctant observer, a second person watching him, and now also listening to him. And what a wretched grunting, cackling, hissing, whining, giggling, screeching he got to hear! These were no primal noises, on the contrary. Only someone from a scary science-fiction story could make such noises, a creature from another planet, certainly not a human being.

The notion of having a spectator and listener who had been standing behind him for a long time and quietly shaking his head was so powerful that he turned to look. No one. Only the tall grasses waving. Nonetheless, the notion persisted. He thought he was still being observed, by someone invisible. That happened to him often, at least once a day, if only for an instant. In different circumstances, the sensation of being seen and heard did him good; it strengthened, clarified—lightened—him; whereas now, on this particular day, in this one moment, it called his entire being into question. It was as if he had been unmasked before the invisible spectator and before the whole world. He was not the person he usually appeared to be, outside of his film roles as well. In no way did he resemble the calm, unflappable, alert person who had things well in hand, the one who almost imperceptibly—see his eyes and lips—accompanied other people and things, supporting them all the more, had merely feigned the calmness and dignity that had caused a person like me, and not only me, to speak of him as 'my actor', in the sense in which one speaks, and not just casually but proudly, and with reference to one's whole life, of 'my teacher', 'my lawyer' (who perhaps never turned up, or never at the right moment), 'my prince' (even if people of that sort died out long ago) or, why not, in another way, yet almost as proudly and as if pertinent to one's entire life, 'my shoemaker', 'my cabinetmaker', 'my doctor', 'my prompter'. . .

To him, it was a fact, not merely a notion: with his flailing around, done so badly and creating such a bad impression on the invisible observer and the entire world, he had betrayed his acting and lost his actor's honour, not for good but for a while, for the next hour, for the way across the clearing, for three paces—but they counted. And he was rid of his profession (as he had almost wished to be, and not for the first time, by the way) at least until the following day and the beginning of the shoot. 'I'm phoney. I'm a phoney.' That sounded as if it were being sung, and in a voice different from the one just heard. It matched his appearance, as did the outstretched arms and the legs planted calmly on the ground. If that did not express serenity, what next?

'I'm a phoney. And the clearing is phoney, too. And the woods are also phoney.' They could make one serene, these disenchantments. Just look: the cherry trees on the edge of the clearing, long since devoid of fruit this summer, with at most a few stems poking out among the leaves, limp as only cherry leaves can be in summertime, with dried-out bare pits dangling from them here and there. And look: the lovely tracklessness of the clearing, with only tall grass far and wide, had also been deceiving. A whole constellation of paths must cross it, becoming recognizable, with the summer's midday sun drying everything, in the clouds of dust whipped up by the motorbikes' heavy tyres, also, to lesser extent, by the cross-country ski poles, and to be heard in the crunching of the gravel with which the network of paths was apparently spread. What had once been a natural clearing, far from everything, now belonged to a forest in proximity to a metropolis, almost a park. If a transition from the trackless area existed, he had not noticed. The former remoteness or wilderness quality did still make itself felt in this world, however. Both seemed to measure themselves against each other and it was as if a competition were under way between the scraping of the crickets and that of the gravel, the screeching of the falcons and that of the bicycle bells. First one would gain the upper hand, then the other. A call and response with a beauty all its own. And in the middle of the clearing, at the centre of the spokes formed by the paths, stood one rather crippled-looking pine tree—how had he managed to overlook it?—stuck in there and out of place in that region of deciduous trees: its boughs draped from top to bottom with chestnut-blossom strings that had blown from the woods nearby—a phoney Christmas tree.

What made the artificial tree unusual did not strike him until he was standing directly in front of it, in the middle of the clearing, at the point where all the paths converged. He had made his way there through the chest-high grass, wading as if defiantly straight through a forest of seemingly unreal stinging nettles—but they were real. Real also the charred circle by the phoney tree, from an Easter bonfire: it could still be felt in the middle of summer, and would be felt into the fall as well. The Eastertide air could still be smelt and intuited, the quintessential air of early morning. From the crossing point, he continued along one of the paths, his thoughts dwelling on another actor, long since dead, who in his last film walks on gravel, saying, 'It's so comforting to walk on gravel.'

As he walked on, an unexpected harmoniousness manifested itself, unexpected after all that had just taken place. But wasn't it typical of him that in crossing from one realm to another, if the first one was a bottleneck, posing an existential threat or at least calling everything into question, he would next experience a widening, with the ground under his feet becoming all the firmer?

A harmoniousness manifested itself and it affected not only him. This particular harmony, flashing into view again for a long second, connected him to the others in the clearing. And the others hardly differed from the figures on the new world stage. Every one of them embodied a role, each entirely distinct from the others, and he embodied a role as well, except that now all the various contrasting, contradictory roles together belonged to one orbit: the orbit of seconds, the orbit of just one second. Whereas previously all these people had appeared in isolation, not connected to the person ahead of or behind them, now, for the duration of a second, one completed the other by virtue of that very distinctness, that very contrast. And he, the misanthrope, his mind focused on his upcoming role as a man who runs amok, harmonized with them.

On this stretch of path, a bicyclist pedalling past snorts snot out of one nostril, and on that stretch over there, a super-slow walker traces figure-eights in the air with a hazel stick. One person pages through his day-planner as he runs, and another glances at the speedometer—or whatever it is—on her upper arm. Over there someone is sitting hidden in the tall grass, reading the *Odyssey,* and someone else is hauling a wheeled suitcase as tall as he is through the sand, and the woman over there is searching for a picnic spot for herself and her five children, two of whom are black. Then there are that person holding a transistor radio to his ear and listening to or ignoring the world news, and the woman stopping to apply mascara, and also the hikers struggling to read their map in the wind, and also the berry-pickers over there, and the lone mushroom-gatherer there, and two or three couples, spooning in the grass, and the enormous black dog running along so quietly, and a raven flying by, very close to the ground: 'Look, the state bird of Alaska.' And he—the one who has joined them all?—moving diagonally past them? 'World harmony,' he said to himself. Then: 'Yet another illusion. But at least this was a stirring one.' And then: 'The last harmony? And after this? What then?'

It was no illusion. Beneath the bluing sky and the clouds drifting past, coming from the ocean or somewhere, the strangers constituted a togetherness. The summery air, the summery wind had no scent, yet it was as if this togetherness could be smelt. It entered one's nose and lent it nostrils. It lingered. That moment exuded authority—and the person who decided and determined to embody it was him. Who else? No one was entitled to serve as an authority but he, our actor.

He did so by changing his gait, instinctively, without employing a particular technique. Similarly, he altered his gaze. How? That, too, will remain unspecified. What will be described: his gait and his gaze—they were disarming and heartening. And his authority caused those strangers by whom he wanted to be greeted to greet him. The greetings came spontaneously, including from someone who just seconds ago had been completely self-absorbed. No one knew or recognized the actor, and yet this was a sort of recognition on both sides, except that he represented authority—although the others' 'greetings to ye' had not a hint of subservience. One could have called it a kind of homage, though paid not to him but to whom? Yes, to whom? And accordingly, he returned every greeting.

Thus my actor received greetings from, among others, a woman on horseback (young and blond); a couple of policemen on foot patrol; a runner with saucer-sized headphones over his ears; a priest in full regalia, with an acolyte in his robe (on their way through the tall grass to deliver last rites?); another actor, studying his lines as he walked back and forth across the clearing; a Balkan prostitute, out to get some fresh air here before her night in the metropolis down below or hiding from her pimp; a man in a wheelchair who kept getting stuck in the gravel; and even the country's president, returning with his retinue to govern or to act, act, eternally act, briefly interrupting his cries of 'active, active, active' to greet the actor, and at the sight of him opening his eyes wide, wider perhaps than he had opened them since his childhood. He, the president, was the only one who startled himself by uttering the greeting first and would have liked to retract it. Would he recognize the actor that evening when he had to confer the award on him? 'No.'

As some of them passed by, walking, jogging, running, riding, they added something to their greeting. 'Back there by the great oak I saw a boletus!' (This from a biker, of all people—why 'of all people'?) 'That was quite a storm this morning, wasn't it?' 'We'll make it home tonight, won't we?' 'Sorry, I mistook you for someone else. No, you are who I thought you were.' 'Not a day for chasing bad guys!' (The two police officers.) One or two started a conversation, talking without expecting an answer, and he listened in silence and went on his way. As he glanced back over his shoulder, he unexpectedly saw children and more children squatting in the tall grass, forming a circle, and he thought, 'The flowers of goodness.' But among them, too, were already bullies. As a small child, Hitler threw rocks at goats.

One of the mushroom-gatherers was wearing earbuds and explained, after he had removed them to say hello, that keeping an eye out for mushrooms and listening to music—especially works by John Cage and Morton Feldman—complemented each other as little else could. An even better accompaniment to looking for summer mushrooms, as he was doing now, was the country-and-western song 'Summer Wine'. A young person had shared this tip with him and he was certain that his example of going out 'mushroom-hunting'— his expression—wearing a music helmet would catch on. He had published a series of articles describing all the new experiences one could have in this way, no, not in a mycology journal but in *Rolling Stone*, and since the articles appeared, young people all over Europe had stopped plaguing fellow passengers on trains and subways with the rustling from their earphones and instead were roaming quietly through the woods with their eyes glued to the ground, listening just as quietly to the few droplets of sound, audible only to them. One form of attentiveness stimulated the other and vice versa, and all the hallucinogenic mushrooms were nothing by comparison and had promptly fallen out of favour.

The berry-picker who called out a greeting from a blackberry thicket on the edge of the clearing, where he had trampled down the brambles without a moment's hesitation, had the cords of his mobile phone's headset dangling past his temples, and from a distance one could already see that, as he picked berries, he was talking non-stop into the microphone suspended near his mouth. He did pause to utter a greeting and, to tell his story, he then stood up from where he was crouching among the canes. He had on a dark suit with wide pinstripes over a white shirt—spattered with blackberry juice—and could have been from the band of commodity traders that had passed by earlier, he, like them, very pale, except for his cheeks, which were flushed bright red from an agitation that seemed to stem less from his talking into the microphone than from something else.

He was a born gatherer, he said. His gathering focused on things that would be useful, for life in general and for survival, on edible and nourishing items. In the past, he had become convinced, influenced in part by others' reactions, that his gathering was a sickness, a compulsion, and he had been ashamed of it. But his gathering was not a compulsion and also not a passion—or, rather, it was one, a passion that allowed him, when he indulged it in the midst of his professional life, to find peace, something he had experienced with no other passion. Two months earlier, the season of the first wild strawberries! A month ago, the raspberry season, with berries smaller but so much sweeter than the unnaturally large cultivated ones (except that from year to year, the blackberry canes were crowding out the delicate raspberries). And now the season for blackberries, the fruits of midsummer, of high summer. True, more and more clear-cutting was taking place in the national forests, or plantations, they might be called—except that in fifty years, no one would be around to see the newly planted oak trees, if they ever managed to grow. Yet in these clear-cut areas, where the sunlight was particularly strong, more and more blackberries—and what blackberries they were! And no one picking, harvesting, squirrelling away those berries, not even the needy migrants from Eastern Europe or elsewhere. He was not the one who should be ashamed, he said. Yet this was no longer a period of excessive abundance, thank goodness. He had given up trying to understand this world and that troubled him not one iota when he was out in the fresh air doing his gathering, completely preoccupied with it.

He saw his gathering as an art form, he said, whose elements were the spirit of discovery, rhythm and dexterity. Each time he reached for a berry among the thorns, he had to consider every move. Being greedy was not necessarily a bad thing when it came to gathering; rather, it was a childlike, joyous impulse, there for the express purpose of being transformed into happiness through the application of dexterity. So, on the one hand, the berries were picked efficiently, in a steady rhythm but, on the other, one at a time, painstakingly, without jerking and pulling, so as not to cause adjacent berries, often the ripest and best, to fall off, landing deep down in the brambles, out of reach. The large berries, by the way, were not necessarily the ripest; their undersides were often still green and would stay that way, not ripening further, and he had discovered that the sweetest berries were to be found not in the sun that blazed down all day on the clear-cut areas but hidden under the leaves, always in shadow—ah, how they would melt in one's mouth, just one such shade-ripened cluster, a gumminess (*sic*) extending far back onto the palate and from there up to just below the cranium. And his gathering was an art form because it represented a kind of harvesting.

In the end, the stockbroker-gatherer crouched down again and gave a demonstration of his art. He picked, or, rather, plucked, the blackberries with both hands, first with his right hand, then with his left, and so forth, but never with both at once, usually reaching from underneath while making sounds with his lips supposed to imitate the pinging of a harp. At intervals, he held up his little container, an old-fashioned enamelled pail decorated with white and blue flowers that he had bought in an antique shop in London's Chelsea district or somewhere. When the harp section ended, he began to dictate numbers into the microphone, in the rhythm of his picking, prefacing each number with the name of a stock company or such, and in-between he explained that his gathering sharpened his sense for numbers. He said they appeared to him as vividly as the berries, gleaming with the gleam of absolute certainty. The sense for numbers gained in this fashion had never misled him, and this would remain the case.

The berry-picker would never emerge from the tangle of brambles. A wasp's nest, grey on grey, hung there out of sight, rocking in the summer breeze as if long since deserted. The moment he bumped against it, a swarm would burst out of this airy hangar and descend on him with ferocious buzzing. Stung hundreds of times on his lips, tongue and throat, he would break off his litany of numbers and crash to the ground amid the thorns, unable to breathe. The thicket would literally close over him, and in that same moment the huge ant heap, teeming with red bodies, at his feet, which were crossed in a terrible cramp, would begin to spread towards his head. No one would notice his disappearance, the way the earth had swallowed him up. He had no relatives, and even if he did . . .

The gatherers in the thickets nearby—contrary to what he had maintained, he had not been the only one, not by a long stretch—would not have noticed his fall. They happened to be the very ones who, he had insisted, had lost the ancient tradition of gathering, migrants from those poor countries and continents that were growing more impoverished by the day. Entire families and tribes were out picking berries in the underbrush along the forest's edge, not only Eastern Europeans but also Asians, usually in the majority, though strangely no Africans, no blacks. They ranged from grandparents, maybe even great-grandparents, down to the smallest children, barely able to grab things or not even old enough to stand and walk, carried in a back sling by fathers, mothers, uncles, aunts, siblings, while here and there a very old person would also be riding on a younger person's back, the two of them forming an unusual picker duo. And these hordes of gatherers had settled in for more than just a day's picking: in the deep grass near the thickets, a campsite had been set up with tents, actually mere pup tents with fire pits outside, if not permanent, at least good for the two or three weeks during which the blackberries would ripen and over-ripen; and along the access road quite close to the campsite, delivery vans were lined up to transport the harvest. Among these gatherers, the one with his head now lying in the ant heap had represented an exception, the elite.

FOUR

As he headed away from the clearing and towards the city, the actor walked the last few steps facing backwards. Several times I had seen him do this when he was taking leave of a place that meant something to him, and not just in his movies, although that happened in every one of them, whether for a longer stretch or a very short one, sometimes almost unobtrusively, like Hitchcock's appearances in his own films, and I wondered whether walking backwards this way, leaving a place while keeping it in sight, might be a new sport he had invented.

'That I am walking backwards now'—here he was talking to himself again—'means that I have wronged the place. "Damned clearing!" I swore at it, seeing, peeping out from behind every leaf amid the foliage along the edges the pistol from *Blow Up*, aimed at someone. In backing out of the place I am trying to ask it to forgive me. Who was it who said kings never learn to walk backwards? A King Backwards-Walker: that's a role I'd like to play!'

The actor said all this inaudibly, expressing it simply though the way he moved, as indeed his walking in general amounted to a variation on speaking. His walking spoke, told a story. That would change, however, in the course of the day that ended with the Great Fall.

On the previous occasions when he had approached the city from its outermost outskirts, he had encountered only one person, and with this person he had established a sort of acquaintance. It had been one of the bush people, and apparently this person, like the rest of those who had removed themselves from society, had taken himself off to God knows where in the meantime. Towards the edge of the forest, where the path turned into a fitness trail, he now came upon him again. He recognized him by the scar running straight across his forehead; otherwise he would have been unrecognizable, even to his mother or his children. At each earlier encounter, the actor had also found the man's face drastically altered. But today there was no face at all to be seen, above all no eyes, although in their place was something that in an autopsy report would be noted as a 'left eye', a 'right eye'. When they first met, this person had struck the actor as uncommonly beautiful for a man. That had to do, among other things, with his dancer-like shyness, not simply that of a forest-dweller. When seen in motion at a distance, the man embodied both shyness and pride. They had never exchanged a word, just registered each other's presence from afar, and that had been the limit of their contact or, rather, one time the actor had gone towards him, whereupon his local acquaintance had promptly, and so elegantly!, made himself scarce—end of meeting.

Nor was he ever seen, in the woods or on the roads nearby, in the company of his fellow forest-dwellers, quite a few of whom lived in small tent villages resembling kraals. One way or the other, he did not look like someone from a tent, and the woman, who, like so many others, kept a sharp eye on him—he often stood motionless for hours at the edge of the forest that bordered her property —said he slept at his mother's every night and she put dinner on the table for him, washed and ironed his clothes and also cut his hair at regular intervals. It was true that every time they met, this vagabond was spotless, in a quince-blossom-white shirt (than which, as mentioned earlier, there is no whiter white) and with freshly pressed creases in his trousers. And nonetheless, every time they met, something else had happened to his acquaintance. Whereas the rest of the bush people, no matter how unkempt they looked, exuded a certain air of indestructibility, as if they were immortal, 'the immortals of the great woods', this man appeared more and more battered, and his face, initially so nobly beautiful, was not merely disfigured—every feature seemed shredded and displaced, his mouth, his nose and especially his eyes.

Until the day in question, they had continued to take each other in from afar, and the other man had remained his local acquaintance, helping to humanize the region, the surroundings, the country for him. In the actor's imagination, the forest vagabond was a Dorian Gray in reverse: it was not he who remained young and beautiful while his portrait in the attic or wherever became more and more mutilated with every debauchery. Rather, a portrait of him existed, who knows where, which showed him as unchangingly young and beautiful, perhaps a few degrees more beautiful with every actual catastrophe that befell his face and figure.

A portrait like that no longer existed. And the man sitting there, smack in the middle of the trail beside a piece of exercise equipment, was no longer the person he knew. No gaze to register the actor, or anything else. And now the actor addressed him for the first time: Could he be of help? The way his former acquaintance sat there, so bedraggled that he could not possibly be more bedraggled, surrounded by his equally bedraggled possessions, they, too, unrecognizable as such, it was clear that he would never be able to stand up without assistance. The only thing that communicated itself to the actor: the man's mother had died. And, again in contrast to his fellow non-fellows, he had never been seen with a dog.

In making his offer of help, the actor had leant over him. Earlier, the man would have proudly and shyly backed away. On this particular day, the only reaction from the figure seated there motionless, legs outstretched, was a billow of incredible stench, a stench just this side of putrefaction. The joggers and bikers seemed to swerve extra-wide around him, and the users of the fitness trail skipped the apparatus next to which he had collapsed. A midsummer day without smells? Now it had its smell. And the actor crouched down by his old friend, let himself fall to the ground beside him, assumed his posture and stretched out his legs like him in the middle of the trail.

The former acquaintance remained expressionless, unless the intensifying stench, coming in repeated waves, could be interpreted as a form of expression. Once before, during his days as a tile-layer, working with his father, the actor had experienced such shock waves. Before laying ceramic tiles in a house, the two of them had had to remove the existing wooden floor, and upon tearing up the boards, had found a crawl space underneath, no, not harbouring a skeleton or such, just filled with rags and scraps, packed in so tightly that no air could penetrate, and when poked from above, they seemed to release gases that blasted into the room, bursts of stench, and for once father and son were in complete agreement: the only thing to do was to get out of there as fast as possible.

But in this situation fleeing was out of the question, impermissible. And besides, the stench could be avoided if one straightened up and tilted one's head way back, with eyes and nose pointing skywards. No more stench, or if there was any, it was confined to the figure sprawled on the ground. High in the sky a field of clouds like ripples in the sand along an ocean; another cloud-field like spatters of spray; and way up there, an airplane ploughing through the cottony trail of an earlier plane, as if in a ship's wake. And here, too, the eagle traced its circles, so close to millions of humans. It was summertime.

A dog barked in one of the gardens on the edge of the forest, and at once a shout issued from his old acquaintance. Somewhere hammering could be heard from inside a house, and again that shout. This continued and eventually it became clear that the shout consisted of words which, translated from the language of that country, meant something like 'Shut up!' or 'Shut your god-damned trap!' The words were bawled from a swollen throat and seemed to be addressed to someone in particular, not necessarily the dog or the hammer-wielder beyond the trees but to some-one in the immediate vicinity. And at the same time, the person being shouted at was not there in the present but at some point in a distant past. It was addressed not to his mother but to a woman nonetheless. So, contrary to expectation, he had once known a woman, had even lived with her. And she had deceived him, had betrayed and abandoned him. And then, out of sorrow and grief at the betrayal of his love, he had taken leave of his senses and vanished into the forest.

His shouts continued, always the same words and at the same volume and pitch, and it was clear that each shout was a response to a sudden noise, a sound. If at first it had seemed that he shouted 'Shut up!' only when a noise intruded on nature from outside the forest, the subsequent shouts made it clear that they could just as well be caused by sounds from inside the forest, sounds of the forest itself. A blackbird warbled: 'Shut your goddamned trap!' A helicopter buzzed overhead: 'Shut up!' Then a child's voice calling to someone: 'Shut up!' A train's whistle: ' . . . !' An empty plastic bag rustling in the underbrush: ' . . . !' Even the most intimate sounds from houses outside the forest; tree sounds; a single note from a fiddle or a harmonica, carried on a summer breeze; two branches overhead rubbing against each other in that same breeze and making a sound like that of a human couple at only the most sacrosanct moments; a single chirp of a cricket—all caused him to bawl: 'Shut your goddamned trap!'—'Ta gueule!' And when everything fell completely silent, as often happens at the height of summer, and stayed silent for a long while, without so much as a whooshing in the foliage, not even a sizzling, silent as if for ever and ever: 'Shut up! Shut up! Shut up!' That made it clear: he wanted to shout himself to death.

The actor next to him played the part of an audience. He fell in with the shouting, nodding to its rhythm, moving his lips silently, as if he were spelling it out. Did this performance of an audience help the man stop? Did it placate him, let him come to his senses and provide, as had happened so often before, a momentary peace, perhaps lingering, such as after the end of a movie? It did not help, not for a moment. His spectatorship was not even registered. The shouter sat or sprawled there and no artistry in the world, certainly not that of the actor-spectator, could help him. The innumerable flies had a better chance as they landed and swarmed around him, and among them, another strange phenomenon, butterflies in all colours of the rainbow, and even stranger, the occasional honey bee perching on his head (or what was left of it), on his shoulders, on his fly, which was held together by a safety pin.

It was also remarkable that the actor's erstwhile friend-by-sight had been more unsightly each time they met while, on the other hand, initially still handsome when housed in the deepest depths of the forest, from one time to the next, he had edged closer to the periphery and thereby to the outskirts of the megalopolis. By now the epitome of unsightliness, he had moved to within earshot (by now sight or any form of visual perception seemed out of the question for him) of houses and streets, such that no sound emanating from them could escape him. Not only lawnmowers and jackhammers but also vacuum cleaners, washing machines and dishwashers inside the houses pressed and pounded directly on his auditory nerves, hissing, rumbling, roaring right beside him, yes, inside him. A slice of bread popped out of the toaster in a house two streets away from the edge of the forest and he promptly bawled at it. And the same thing happened when a furnace switched on in a cellar somewhere, when a hedge trimmer, not even a power trimmer, snipped away—maybe it was only a bird chirping—when a bike dynamo hummed far off in the night, when even farther off in the nocturnal stillness a key crunched in the lock of a garden gate, a crunching that could also be a hedgehog coughing by his feet. Every sound from the human world made him cry out against it— against whom or what? Against, against, against. It was a cry of pain, and even more of defencelessness. Defenceless, defenceless, defenceless. And at the same time, he had moved towards whatever it was that tormented him, going from one spot to the next, out of the forest, of his own free will, the only decision still available to him.

The spot by the fitness trail would not be his very last. He would not move voluntarily but the mounted forest police, summoned by the community watch group of those who lived near the forest's edge and were annoyed by the shouts ringing out day and night, would pick him up and deposit him on the next best road they came to. And there he would sit, his pile of junk beside him, in a gutter or such, visible to all, no longer hidden by underbrush, and would hold his tongue. Not another cry from his throat, no more 'Shut up!'-s from his lips. And one morning or one evening, he, too, would be gone, his spot in the gutter by the first cash machine vacant. And some of the residents would even miss the shouter. 'What happened to our shouter?' they would wonder. 'He can't have given up, can he? He can't have simply kicked the bucket without another word!'

Did that mean the actor's acquaintance-by-sight would never get up from his spot along the fitness trail? But no, there he was, standing; and, far from struggling to his feet, he had jumped up. The shouter had jumped up and now hurled himself at the exercise apparatus on the trail along the forest edge. But if he planned to knock it over or smash it, he had picked the wrong object. It was a thick tree trunk stripped of its bark and bolted almost a metre off the ground to vertical posts, almost equally thick, to form a balance beam. There was no way to rock it, no way to budge it. Although he hurled himself at it time and again, ramming it with his hands and his shoulders, then with his feet, he could not get the trunk to so much as quiver. It was not entirely the fault of the apparatus. The shouter

—who was not shouting any more, by the way—attacked it without strength. At first it was unclear whether he had none or whether he was not really serious and did not quite have the nerve.

But then it did become clear: he was not giving it his all, did not have the nerve. He was and remained a mama's boy—his mama's boy. And that became evident when the actor stopped serving as his spectator and jumped up too, hurling himself at the balance beam but with all his might. The force with which he ran at the tree trunk, leading with his shoulder, was so great that the impact knocked him over backwards and to the ground.

He did not accomplish anything either. Nonetheless, he scrambled to his feet, this, too, no act, and hurled himself at the apparatus again and then again. As soon as his old acquaintance began to copy him, the shouter had ceased his attacks. He froze in mid-career and, for the first time in what seemed like an eternity, his face showed some expression.

As he attacked the beam with greater and greater force, the actor registered the shouter's behaviour only out of the corner of his eye, but, as often happens, this kind of perception captured something meaningful. What he saw was the forest-dweller's childhood face, a face that had never actually existed. In the case of the many lost souls to whom the actor felt drawn, he had often felt compelled to imagine their faces from earlier, from their childhood, but never had he succeeded before in seeing one of them as an actual child (with the others, it sometimes worked as they lay dying). But there it was now, the image—and gone already. A child's face revealed itself for the first time in the other man, even if he was not aware of it. Or was he after all?

It, the face, had appeared as a result of profound shock. And the bush-dweller had received that shock from the man next to him, who, unlike him, had been completely serious in his display of violence, in his attempt to knock over the balance beam. That had not been the man's intention. In charging the beam, he had had nothing in mind at all, and if he had had anything in mind, it was forgotten in his shock at the other man's seriousness. He, the forest idiot, was incapable of violent behaviour and had never harmed a hair on anyone's head, which perhaps explained why he had become an outcast. And his shock at this man, embodying all the violence in the world, went hand in hand with a desire to appease him. His helpless shock, combined with the equally helpless desire to appease, brought his child-face to the surface. There he stood, letting himself be seen, his hands partly raised in a gesture of appeasement.

The actor responded by breaking off his attempt and moved on to something else. He gave a demonstration of balancing for the other man's benefit, not on the balance beam but on a tree trunk next to it that had been uprooted in the last storm. But the bush-dweller was no longer able to take it in. No trace of the child-face left, or of any face at all. The other man's balancing, albeit so much more natural than that of a fitness-trail-user who was teetering at the same time along the raised beam—childish foolishness (if he even noticed). And as the actor headed off down the road, shouts rang out again, at top volume: 'Shut your goddamned trap!'

The actor found himself uttering that very exclamation out under the open sky, as he took the first steps that led away from the forest. His 'Shut your goddamned trap!' came out almost inaudibly and he was not merely mimicking his erstwhile acquaintance. As often happened to him, for a brief interval, he had become the other person, without intending to. Just as people had once said, 'Sean Connery *is* James Bond,' 'Sylvester Stallone *is* Rocky,' 'Henry Fonda *is* the young Mr Lincoln,' 'Peter Lorre *is* M,' it could be said of him, 'X *is* that other person.' And this, too, applied more to his life outside of films than to the parts he played. And the person he became was never ever someone happy or victorious or triumphant but usually someone like the man he had just left behind. What saved him from crashing and burning: he never became the other person for more than a second. 'Saved up to now.' (Spoken to himself again.)

While embodying the other man he was blind —though not deaf—to the metropolis in the valley below and to the horizons, the distant and most distant ones, beyond which the city stretched farther and farther. His only horizon at the moment consisted of the shoes on his feet. The lace on one shoe had come undone and, as the other man, he would never again bend down to tie it. As he dragged himself along, the other shoe would come undone and he would leave it that way until at some point he would trip over the laces and fall to the ground head first, never to get up again. While embodying the other man, he felt the keys to his house, a two-hour flight from there, as an unfamiliar object in his trouser pocket and would kick them into the first catch-basin he came upon, along with his credit cards and his mobile phone ('Disgraceful that I carry that thing around, and besides, it weighs down my jacket!'). He would take off his jacket and, with it, his necktie, and toss them over the hedge bordering a suburban garden. He would strip to his bare skin and sit down on a nearby hydrant, wearing nothing but his rustic hat with the falcon feathers. Even the other man's stench there in the underbrush would have transferred itself to him and would billow around him so revoltingly that the passers-by—why were there none?—would give the naked man a wide berth, as the fitness runners had done with the other man.

The actor stuck his hand in his pocket, reaching for his key chain, and it would have taken very little for him to actually toss it into a ditch or into one of the suburban dustbins lined up along the pavement. But as always, from back in his days as a tile-layer, he had so much stuff in his pockets that it was a good while before he located the keys, and, when he finally found them, it took a lot of pulling and shaking to get the hand holding them out of his pocket, and by then, fortunately, the 'other person's moment' had passed—why 'fortunately'? — 'at least in this case'.

The hand stuck in the trouser pocket reminded the actor of the book he had been reading that morning in the woman's house. The hero of the story had experienced something similar: after surviving, more or less successfully, the adventure with the lemon seed that kept eluding his grasp, once out on the road he had put his hand in his pocket for no particular reason and it had got stuck, and when the reader had closed the book after a few more pages, that hand was still stuck in that pocket. And next the actor recalled the film that was supposed to be shot all around the city, starting the next day, with him as the main character, someone who ran amok, more wildly and ferociously at war with the world than Robert de

Niro's taxi driver, and, like the exclamation 'Shut your goddamned trap!' moments before, he now heard himself saying, 'I shan't make that film. I shan't even quit, I will simply not show up. And I shan't go to the award ceremony this evening either.'

Did he really mean that? No. As usual, he was just talking to himself. Yet he immediately wanted to take it back. 'I mustn't talk this way. I forbid myself to say such things. Except that forbidding oneself doesn't work—has no effect. Someone else has to forbid me. But who?'

At his feet, beyond the horizon of his shoes, beneath the summery sky, now a delicate blue, evocative of the sea, after the morning thunderstorm, the city lay spread out before him. It was the entire city, although it continued on the plateaus beyond the hills in the distance, and it lay there, with districts where clusters of skyscrapers crowded together, and massive single office buildings towering here and there. It was not the clear air and the light alone that made the city appear beautiful. It was beautiful in itself, in its seemingly natural grandeur and its architectural patchwork, which balanced each other. The light reinforced the predominant white colouration and softened it here and there, just as it subordinated the scattered dark and decidedly taller buildings to the more numerous smaller white ones. From where he stood, hardly any motion or any sound could be detected, and yet a rhythm communicated itself to him from down below, quiet and steady. A number of cities in the world aspired to be recognized as the city of cities. This one deserved that distinction, at least for the current moment, and what was more worth savouring than this moment?

The actor bent down and tied his shoelace. He also tightened his necktie, dampened his index finger with the tip of his tongue and ran it along the brim of his rustic hat. Having stepped out of the forest onto the road, here on the threshold of the city he brushed the mud off his soles, hopping from one leg to the other, as one knocks the snow off one's boots in wintertime before coming indoors —and scratched and rubbed, using rain water from a puddle, the patches of forest dirt off his suit—when it came to spots and the like on his clothing, he was very particular, unlike with torn or threadbare patches. Finally, he carefully tucked his shirt into his trousers and, as he did so, he had an image of himself playing a man in a film who was condemned to death. This man, wearing dark trousers and a white shirt, had tucked in his shirt in just this way as he stepped before the firing squad. And that condemned man had not escaped.

Why did an image like that pop up at the very moment when he was about to head down into the city? Nothing could compare with a city like that. Not a trace of haze. In the river basin, the air seemed to be just as clean as up here on the plateau. No factory smokestacks anywhere for a long time now, and the deceptively bright smoke from the refuse incinerators: long since cleaned up. And other things whose absence pleased him even more: nothing green met the eye among all the little cubes of white, no parks interrupted the rhythm. Even in his childhood—something he had certainly had, despite his motherlessness—he had never cared for parks. (But a forest, by contrast, or forests altogether!) No park in sight: fine by him. Cemeteries at his feet, however, that was fine, too, as many as possible, clearly visible from east to west, from north to south, and along the diagonals, even smaller white patches inserted into the seemingly endless white patchwork, fragments of a cross that stretched over the globe, in the south and west, the north and east.

He pulled his shirt out from under his belt again. As he walked, the shirt-tails would have worked their way out in any case and flapped over his hips. No shouter to be heard in the woods behind him, or he no longer listened for him. Facing backwards again, the actor took his first steps towards the city. Strange to say, it felt as if he had not passed through the forest just recently but an eternity ago, or never.

And likewise, the city had seemed very close just now, to be reached and crossed beneath the summery firmament as if he had wings on his feet, without any need for seven-league boots. But almost at once, as he came upon the first houses, all of them low to the ground, a premonition, followed by certainty, that it would take him a long time to reach the city below, enter it and possibly pass through it, and the journey would be more than long—it would be arduous, unsure and challenging, a veritable expedition. That realization gave him such a jolt or a push that for the steps that followed, he did something else he had forbidden himself to do: he ran. And as he ran, hunger overcame him, a first immense, undefined, lifelong hunger, then a small, specific first hunger, for food. But since experience had taught him that this kind of sudden, searing hunger was not the real thing and would soon pass, he forbade himself to give in to it. Another of his self-prohibitions . . .

As he gradually made his way down towards it, the metropolis seemed to spread farther and farther, as if it would never end, either in the west at the ocean, where it encompassed innumerable ships, boats, tankers and aircraft carriers, or in the east, where it merged into and up over the Alps, with lifts on even the smallest slopes, still in operation now, in summer, day-in, day-out, though without the clatter of skis. If the city ended anywhere, extending its very last tentacle, it was here, behind him, on the edge of the forest. On the other hand, all the sounds so clearly audible in the forest had fallen silent or been muffled, simply as a result of his stepping out into the open and heading towards them, just as cicadas promptly cease their shrilling when one approaches, and a choir of crickets, when one enters its orbit, lowers its chirping to the very limit of audibility, as if a volume dial has been turned down as far as it will go. Thus the railroad tracks and switches, from which a veritable racket could be heard in the woods whenever a train passed, made no noise at all—had rail traffic been suspended from one moment to the next? And announcements on the loudspeaker at the nearby station which had echoed through the forest like bellowing—causing the forest-dweller to bellow in response—now produced only a kind of background noise amid the rustling of the silence as he stepped into the open. Was the voice even making announcements, or was he still hearing the almost violent top-decibel shouting from earlier as it ebbed away in his ear, from where it had made its way into his head and there into the most sensitive circuits of the brain? For the duration of one more step, the actor became the other person again. But no: the sounds now so distant formed part of the silence, which took on a life here among the small houses very different from the silence among the trees in the forest and valuable in its own way. And the barking of dogs also sounded so distant, as if coming from farmsteads located far apart in the countryside, 'in the plain of the ancient river,' the actor said to himself. That was where he came from. And upon hearing such barking, he felt as though it were evening already and he had successfully made it this far. 'Why "made it"?'

The sole person to cross his path as he began his passage through the last recognized outskirts of the metropolis—he did not go straight but, rather, wove back and forth—was a jogger or, rather, a runner. Upon catching sight of him along a slight decline in the road, the actor made a bet with himself: by noticeably slowing his pace, as he always did when someone else, especially a crowd, sped up, he would force the other to follow his example. He lost this bet, as almost always happened, and that embittered him at first but then cheered him up.

Later it was couples who came towards him, couples of a new kind such as the world had seldom seen before the time in which this story takes place, or at least not in such numbers. These couples could be found all across Europe, in the snow, under palm trees, in the rearmost of rear courtyards, in pitch blackness, in broad daylight. And now they appeared in swarms, as if concentrated in this border area, almost free of passing cars because of the summer holidays. (Cars were parked here and there but they seemed not to have been driven for a long time—with bird droppings and rain streaks on their windshields and roofs—not a few of them under tarpaulins that billowed in the borderland breezes.) Each of the couples consisted of one ancient person and one much younger person, usually in the bloom of youth. They seemed rooted to the spot, yet somehow they did move, almost imperceptibly, at intervals between which an almost interminable hesitation inserted itself, after which progress might never occur again, in any direction whatsoever. And in the silent streets, they could be heard from a long way off before they ever so gradually came into view, little by little. Only the old man or the old woman could be heard, however, and that solely from the clumping that accompanied their approach, as if someone were pounding along on the heaviest lead soles, more like chunks of lead, a different kind of Frankenstein's monster, a massive King Kong.

The couples hesitated as he came abreast of them, and it was always the old man or the old woman who was responsible. Arm in arm with the younger one, or, rather, supported by the younger one, the oldsters would decide, upon catching sight of the actor approaching, that this was it—out of the question that they should continue setting one foot in front of the other. That amounted to a decision, the only one of which they were still capable, and it filled them with something like cheerfulness. If a few steps back, steps that consisted more of tottering along under duress, their expression, if any, had been thoroughly grouchy, now, at the moment in which they had resolved never to stir from the spot again, they beamed at him, the third party, as impudently and cheekily as only old people can when, helpless or in the clutches of dull despair, they reach a decision firmer than ever before, finally finding a solution, the only and last possible solution. Yes, from now on and from this spot, they would not budge, either to continue or to return home, wherever that was—they had forgotten anyway, as they had forgotten everything else. Their decision had become possible because of him, the single passer-by on the summery streets, otherwise peopled only by couples like theirs, and all forming side streets to side streets to still other side streets. And he was the witness to their decision. Their gazes at him, beaming from deep within, were furthermore those of rogues, asking the heavens or someone to forgive them for this roguish act—not another step!—or merely seeming to do so.

Whenever he glanced back at them over his shoulder, they had allowed their young partners to persuade them after all to resume tottering, scuffing, hobbling along. 'Just a few more steps, and now another step for . . . and now one for . . . and one for . . . ' And as he went on his way, zigging and zagging, sometimes heading away from rather than towards the centre, on every street he ran into another such couple, the elderly partner, if not silent then audible from afar moaning and groaning, the young one offering encouragement, glancing at a watch or other timepiece and finally issuing commands, often in an almost incomprehensible accent or a very foreign language.

The actor came upon one of the couples seated on a bench by an otherwise unoccupied—how else could it be?—bus stop. At first he assumed the two of them were waiting for the bus and greeted them as he passed. Not until he received no response, and none when he repeated his greeting, did he pull up short and look more closely. Sitting there, resting from making its rounds for hours or weeks among the silent houses on the outskirts, was another couple, but not a typical one. The 'ancient' one, a man, was not all that old, had dark hair with only a few streaks of grey, and a smooth face, slightly flushed, perhaps from medication, while the 'young' one, a woman, seemed hardly younger and was wearing a dress of a material such as was worn in these parts almost exclusively by migrants from the most poverty-stricken lands to the east, and also dirty, which the actor noticed immediately (see above), as he also noticed the warts on her face and the hairs sprouting from them.

The only thing to do was to look the other way and continue: nothing to be seen here. And in that moment, he realized that he knew the man hunched up on the bus bench who was staring right through him—and not only him here. The realization came to him in a flash, with a clarity possible only in the case of something he would never ever have considered likely to occur. The stranger here, in a strange land, had once been his neighbour in the country they both called their own, and a good neighbour. Almost a friend. A friend. Uttering an exclamation, the actor wheeled around, saying his name, 'Andreas!'—the first name that had come to the actor's mind that day and crossed his lips. From the beginning the woman had been only 'the woman' to him—which had been, could have been, an expression of deep respect in the region from which he came; and on this day, his faraway son had been simply his son, or only 'the son'.

No reaction from the man he had called by name. Confirmation came, however, in response to his repeating the first name and adding the last name in the form of a question, from the woman sharing the bench, in a hodgepodge of at least three languages. Yes, he was the one. And this Andreas was done for. 'You won't get anything out of him. Say what you will, he won't take it in. It's all over with him. Finito!' And as he gazed at the other man, the actor suddenly recalled their shared past: as a result of their very different callings in life—he had never been able to picture someone very similar to himself as a neighbour or friend—they had become close, good neighbours, which for a while counted as much as a friendship. He had even felt the other man to be a kindred spirit, this strengthened in turn by their professions, which outwardly had next to nothing in common. With this Andreas the actor had felt more at home than in the company of people familiar to him from childhood, and not only because of his earlier life as a tile-layer. But the so-called regular folks, with whom he got along splendidly, seemed die out in the course of the years. (Or had they never really existed? No, they had!) And so he had let himself be taken by surprise, after initial resistance to his new neighbour, who, as a man of commerce, as he was said to be, represented someone not entirely without power. 'He surprises me,' he said quietly to himself, and in that spirit things could go well between the two of them.

The other man, experienced in business, had no need to be taken by surprise when it came to making common cause with his neighbour, at the time already a respected actor. 'He always saw eye to eye with me immediately.' Andreas had none of the common prejudices against actors. He took the profession seriously, just as he took all professions seriously, at least whenever possible, as part of being in business. Furthermore, he expected something of the actor every time they met, as if the actor knew something he did not, something of use to him in his work, and not only needed but needed urgently, as a matter of life and death. Yet he had never seen his neighbour act, not even once, either in a film or on the stage (certainly not there). He simply knew who he was, and to see him standing, walking and sitting in the garden next door had been enough to give him a boost.

As time passed, Andreas invited himself over to his neighbour's more and more often. He was a stranger in town like him, the actor, and lived alone. His wife worked for the same firm but in a different country, or perhaps there was no wife—the things he told his neighbour about her seemed on the one hand very concrete, on the other hand rather like a fairy tale. Towards the end of their acquaintance, these visits increasingly struck the actor as uncanny. His neighbour turned up more and more often without notice, appearing outside the garden gate shortly before midnight and, without ringing the bell, he would shout to him in the house, after which they would sit together indoors without speaking, the actor waiting patiently, the other man appearing more intense every evening and, so it seemed, more needy, as if at the site of an oracle from which an utterance was to issue forth—now, now, please—that would relieve him of making a decision that would affect either his entire existence or only the following morning.

During these pre-midnight visits, the neighbour would edge his chair closer and closer to the actor. That began to feel like a threat, yet it was really nothing more than a frantic plea for guidance, legible in the man's wide eyes in the stillness of night. His utter bewilderment could be smelt—that was how close he came—a foul odour from his half-open mouth. 'But I never knew what advice to give him—at most I tried to distract him with trivial matters, calling his attention to the night wind blowing through our gardens or a blue ball caught in the fork of a tree, or comparing the capacity of our heating-oil tanks.' Anything but mention the next day, or speak of 'the future'. And for a while, he even listened to the inconsequential remarks, nodding as if they were the oracle, thanked his neighbour and went on his way. Later he just stared at the actor as he gave voice to these distractions and allowed him, without a word of thanks, or any word at all, to walk him home, until their relationship ended when Andreas, the business expert, was reassigned to Mongolia where, to judge by what was reported, his work made a difference.

Since then his friend the actor had heard nothing from him and he seemed to have disappeared altogether; no one had any news of him, either from the newspaper or from any message, and the actor, who thought of him time and again —and just this morning, as he now realized, had thought of him intensely for a second—had never been able to imagine anything other than his vanishing without a trace into the Gobi Desert. Otherwise he would have let himself be heard from, and if by no one else then at least by him, his good neighbour of many years. 'Hallo, neighbour, I'm back!'

So here he was again. Except that he was not resuming contact. And although he gazed at the actor wide-eyed, those eyes wider than ever, which made it look as if his whole face were laughing, albeit without any sound of laughter, and then even began to speak, in no way did this equate to being seen or heard by him. Or might it after all? Might it? What he uttered were no complete sentences, nothing but isolated words, or words trying to be sentences. Trying? Yes, it appeared that some desire remained, or what was left of it. He barely moved his lips and his voice, which had once almost boomed from one garden to the other, became more inaudible with every word he spoke, each coming out more tonelessly than the last, and yet the desire, the urgency, the effort to speak seemed to increase, in a way familiar to the actor from scenes in films, especially in Westerns, which portrayed the dying.

He began with nouns and eventually moved on to verbs and other parts of speech: ' . . . snowball fight . . . blackboard . . . defenestration . . . dragonflies . . . early apples . . . temple-hopping . . . gas masks . . . hand grenades . . . Hitler . . . knee-raising . . . money-changing . . . raspberries . . . face-slaps . . . money or life . . . hill and dale . . . so green . . . so dear . . . turn back . . . go home . . . '

He spoke the last two words three times, then fell silent, after which he continued to gaze at the actor wide-eyed, as if he were to blame for everything and at the same time the one person he had waited for all this time, not for help—that was an utter impossibility—but so that he could say to him, the one responsible, the things he had just said, face to face. The actor, for his part, although Andreas obviously did not recognize him, and certainly not as his erstwhile neighbour, knew that he was meant, he and he alone, and in his innermost self, as himself, and that he now had to withstand this gaze and, furthermore, find a response to those words, the only right one; otherwise he would have failed and the day would go awry; if he were a failure, it would extend beyond that day. This was no game such as two children might play or might have played at one time—we stare into each other's eyes and the one who blinks first or looks away loses: this was serious. Much was at stake. It was a test. And in the balance were the actor's eyes, which until today at least had always provided an adequate response, an adequate answer. Woe unto him if he could not hold his own against the other man's gaze. He would see himself for ever after as a fraud.

It did not come to the decisive moment, 'not yet,' he told himself afterwards. The woman on the bench by the bus stop plucked at the sleeve of her patient's windbreaker—if indeed Andreas was her patient, which his friend did not want to believe— then grabbed it and tugged: a sign that the bus was approaching. Get up! Get ready to board the bus!—whereupon the actor had to move out of the way, moved to one side and, without consciously deciding to, continued his journey. When he paused after a few paces to wave to the passengers on the bus, it drove by completely empty, empty as buses

can be only at the height of summer on the outskirts of major cities. So he was still walking
through outskirts . . . And as he glanced over his
shoulder, the couple had not left the bus shelter, the
woman standing, his former neighbour seated, not
to be budged from the spot, no matter what. The
only sign of movement: the wind puffing out his
windbreaker.

For a second, the actor almost turned back—
which brought to mind how often on this day he
had toyed with turning back ('anywhere but to the
city, anywhere but to the centre')—to push the
nurse, or whatever she was, aside, to sit down on
the bench next to the other man and, like him, to
refuse to let anything in the world dislodge him
from the spot. And at the same time, this fantasy:
if he did that, the foreign woman would promptly
turn into a monster, and Andreas and he would be
done for. This fantasy offered no details, making
its effect all the more powerful—even more powerful as pure fantasy than any thought and any
specific image. And so he kept going, walking fast.
He almost broke into a run, which would have
resulted in his being immediately disqualified in
his obstacle-course sport.

My actor had been inclined from childhood to
keep his head down. His time as a tile-layer had

reinforced this proclivity. It seemed to him that he was meant to look down at the ground; to look up at the sky, he had to pull himself together mightily, and in his films he tended to squint when he looked up, which proved particularly effective with audiences. But now, as he put distance between himself and that helpless figure, feeling helpless himself, he involuntarily raised his head, in a sort of rage. In the otherwise blue summery sky, a single trail of thick, snow-white clouds: clumps of snow, left behind from the soles of someone who had come stomping out of the snowy region over the horizon and already disappeared over the other horizon—the soles of a snow-hiker. 'Bow your head, friend!'

It seemed as though his gazing at the ground and his wanting to help went together—helping was his natural inclination. Helping, him, an actor? 'Yes.' Like his lowered head, helping had been his inclination from the time he was small. Except that his desire to help took a form different from the no less intense desire manifested by certain of his prominent colleagues from 'film and television'. He had no interest in taking a political stand, in making a sharp distinction between the good people who deserved help and the bad people who did not. Altogether, he cared not at all about helping the multitudes, communities, peoples, including peoples from the third and countless other worlds. Those he felt compelled to help were individuals, whether poor or rich, whether total strangers or neglected neighbours, whose deprivation and despair were not widely known, had first to be discovered.

When he came upon such a case, it seemed to him that the most natural thing was not merely to help but, if possible, to save the person in question. Had he actually saved anyone? True, the parts he played had never been those of saviours like El Cid or Don Juan (Molière's, who saved, for instance, the brother of one of his sweethearts). Yet he heard from many in his audiences that he had helped them, had even saved their lives, through his acting —however that might be. 'You've saved my life time and again,' people wrote to him, or simply, 'You gave me back my peace of mind,' 'You reminded me what I once dreamt of doing,' whereupon these audience members usually added a personal wish: one of them wanted to play football with him some day, a second one hoped to spend a few days hiking with him; a third man or woman wanted to 'cook for' him or cut his hair. And now it occurred to him that the stream of expressions of gratitude and thank-you notes had dwindled and, finally, almost dried up entirely. Because no one else wanted to be saved, at least not by a film and an actor? Because no one and nothing could be saved any more? Or simply because people did not write letters these days?

And it occurred to him furthermore that outside of his work as an actor, in his everyday life, he had not managed to this day to save a single person. True, he had constantly been on the verge of diving into water, dashing into flames, jumping down onto tracks in the underground to pull to safety someone who had fallen into the path of an oncoming train. But he had always fallen short—grabbing someone by the belt who had ended up perilously close to the rails was not the same as saving the person, nor was carrying a woman to land when she was trapped on a sandbar and about to be swept away by the rising tide, or diving, rather melodramatically, for his son one time when the little boy suddenly lost his footing in an Alpine lake.

On closer inspection, this kind of literal intervention was not what he had in mind in any case. He thought of himself more as a spiritual saviour. He felt capable of serving as a saviour of souls if need be. At the decisive moment he could, of that he was certain, pull any person in despair, anyone to whom the words 'Over, it's all over' applied, back to a perch, a shaky one, true, but safe for the time being, and to do so without undertaking any obvious action, also without words, also without a look—though a look was more likely—simply by showing up, as himself, by being there. And although in reality, away from films, he had not yet had this effect—one time in the underground, he had quietly taken a seat next to an evidently unhappy person who had jerked away from him in horror, rendered unreachable in his unhappiness by fear—he could not be deterred from his conviction that he was a saviour. His woman in Alaska had once remarked, 'You seem to see yourself as an angel.' To which my actor replied, 'Although I've never played one, and never could, and although, as I said, I've never really saved a person—yes.' Merely helping did not suffice; merely helping could be a kind of betrayal. Saving was what mattered!

'At most, I have saved animals thus far, and only quite small ones. The largest animal was a ram whom I pulled by his horns out of a burning barn, but my saving him was a swindle—the minute I had to let go of his horns because the heat had become unbearable, the ram, who had been digging in his heels up to then, dashed into the open on his own. It's curious, though, that intervening on behalf of small and tiny creatures has preoccupied me for years and that in this regard I see myself as a saviour. Once I hiked for days through one of the deserts, of which there are more and more in these days in Europe, without running into a single human soul or any animal, not even a bird, until in the evening I came upon a bee. It had just fallen into a trough left behind in the desert from the days when it was still a pasture and was now filled with rainwater, and the bee was spinning around for dear life; I became this bee's saviour. And likewise, on a different hike, I saved a hedgehog I came upon in a forest that had turned into a wilderness; the hedgehog's snout, or whatever a hedgehog's nose is called, had got caught in a rusty fence overgrown with vines, and the animal could not move backwards or forwards in spite of being there for days, pushing and pulling, and now it had next to no strength left. I saved it by cutting the wire, if memory serves: the saviour, the angel, for a hedgehog and a bee.'

And now he had just missed an opportunity to save a human being by intervening, by sitting down silently between his friend and the strange woman who had him under an evil spell. Even if all the doctors in the world had proclaimed that someone this ill could not be saved, he was certain it was possible—it would have been possible through him, the good neighbour.

He paused. Could he turn back, in spite of the off-limits zone created by the witch? But it was too late to rescue the man and return him to the world beneath the big sky, to the current moment; the time for that had passed, once and for all. Nonetheless, he could feel strength, unchannelled and all the more unruly, surging through him. The next time around, he would give it its head, at just the right moment—and that would happen today, this very day.

SIX

Like signals meant expressly for him, more and more ambulances could be heard, likewise police sirens, but all from a distance and from down below in the city. 'You've zigged and zagged enough now; it's time to forge full speed ahead, to get moving; that's where it's happening, in the centre, not up here in these depopulated outskirts, abandoned by God and the world, and even by hedgehogs and bees!'

Going straight ahead turned out to be impossible, however—for that one would have had to fly, in one of the helicopters, for instance, of which increasing numbers were in evidence, following not just one flight path but more and more. The few straight streets either terminated at railway embankments or proved deceptive, taking one in a circle, especially in the new housing developments, laid out in such a way that each formed a loop. He would have needed a very detailed map to find the one, almost secret, way out of the spirals. But at first he felt he halfway knew the city from earlier visits, and was in the mood to find his way without a plan, besides which he almost liked going astray in the process; he thought he would gain something as a result. And furthermore, all the outlying and in-between districts turned out to be quite densely populated, by humans as well as animals, at least for an hour during which the great midsummer desertedness outside of the centre ceased to be in effect, first imperceptibly, then all at once.

Gradually, the couples made up of ancients and their youthful partners gave way to figures whom one could not possibly see as couples, no matter how one tried. Either they were individuals, their numbers, too, increasing like those of the ambulances, or entire swarms of insects, birds, four-legged creatures, two-legged creatures. The two doves from earlier, flying from roof to roof, the quintessential peaceable couple, were followed by hordes of crows, not summery in the slightest, pursuing smaller birds and refusing to let anyone shoo them away when they attacked a single sparrow or woodpecker and left it dying, stabbed by their beaks, in the gutter; they cawed as menacingly as Hitchcock's demonic seagulls at anyone who got in their way. What bit him on the hand, the throat and the neck were no wasps or other stinging insects but swarms of delicate, seemingly fragile, almost transparent grasshoppers. And it was hardly an exaggeration to say that in this hour, the butterflies that had earlier fluttered back and forth in pairs now came together en masse and dive-bombed not only him but anything that protruded from the ground—even blades of grass and pebbles, as if the butterflies had become the enemies of inanimate objects as well.

Now the school playgrounds were also filled, although school was out for the summer and would remain so for a good while. All the children were running around, directed by their caretakers' shouts, in the paved but sometimes also grassy playgrounds surrounded by high fences, where they were spending a good part of their holidays, or all of them. And one could bet—and this bet with himself he won—that behind each of these fences, along the side that bordered on the street, one child stood alone, apart from the others, and often it was a black child; indeed black children accounted for the great majority on these playgrounds. Such a child, one could also bet, would be poking its hands through the mesh of the fence, trying to catch the eye of passers-by. (This bet, however, was less of a sure thing.) The third bet he lost time after time: upon the actor's looking through the fence, not looking at the child, let alone smiling at him, the child would smile, gazing to one side or smiling to himself. It even happened that the young loner spat at him, as if waiting for the chance. Except that the spittle he had collected in his mouth in advance had become so thick that it got caught in the wire mesh or ricocheted onto the spitter (there was also a little girl spitter).

Others out and about alone were the ancient folk, stopping to rest on some of the benches along the street as they made their way home from unseen supermarkets, their little shopping carts full. All the benches were positioned in such a way that they faced a wall, if anything, never offering a view into the distance, down towards the city and out towards the horizons. These elderly people, of whom more and more appeared, trembled all over, their heads wobbling—although some did not tremble as they sat there quietly, their eyes closed—and from time to time they sighed in an almost friendly way, as if amused at themselves. Heard all at once from bench to bench and from street to street, the sighs would have constituted a chorus or a canon. And this canon would have gone as follows: 'I—and I—and I am on my last, or next to last, outing. I want to take advantage of it and stay here outside for a bit. How lonely and tired I am. How pointlessly the helicopters buzz overhead. Yet another state visit, and another.

And only a little while ago I was a child, isn't that odd? I'm shaking my head, stranger, it's not wobbling. And my trembling is not merely the tremor of old age. Will I be able to find the key hole and turn the key with my arthritic hand? Will I get the refrigerator open? Will I make it to the toilet? And that summer you and I spent together! Ah, Summer Wine. Summer in the City! Summertime Blues . . . '

As if in a pre-established rhythm, in that transitional district, the isolated individuals were followed by dense crowds of people, packs that had formed here and there, or that was how it looked to the actor. Thus, on an otherwise deserted summery street, he came upon a gang of adolescents whose eyes told him they were up to no good. They were brandishing clubs and it seemed advisable to get out of their way. But such a move might provoke them, so, instead of trying to avoid them, he moved even more slowly than before, wending his way through the group, and behold, the gang, if it had even aspired to be one, split up, and one of the youths, seemingly to his own surprise, greeted him, while the young man next to him exclaimed, 'Look, a crusader!' and the only girl among them—such 'gangs' always had one girl, just one, usually bolder than the boys and not just putting it on—looked him in the eye and said, 'You're going in the wrong direction, stranger.' The clubs the boys made whistle through the quiet air were baseball bats, known in the press as lethal weapons, but, as became clear only on closer inspection, the youths were also carrying the appropriate gloves and balls. How often this had happened to my actor: the first impression grew out of a preconception and blocked a possible closer look. As an instructor at a school of acting— 'Lord, preserve me!'—he would have emphasized to his students the importance of taking a second look.

After the gang, on another summery street, he came upon an individual engaged in unlocking a front door. This was not someone almost a hundred years old but a young man. At first nothing about him seemed unusual except that he was fumbling with an enormous bunch of keys, odd for the kind of one-storey cottage typical of the outskirts and suburbs. The bunch of keys rattled in the silence all around as if it were competing with the helicopters high overhead. He tried key after key, without success. This could have been a stock scene from a Charlie Chaplin or Jacques Tati film, the more so as the man swayed and teetered and bobbed, seemingly drunk as a skunk, as he flipped through the keys. Upon closer inspection, however, he was not drunk. He just failed time and again to get into his house, for whatever reason. Even if he found the right key, he would not manage, not today and not tomorrow. And no one inside the house who might have let him in, for he lived alone there—had lived there until the present moment. If only he could collapse, to put an end to his struggle to get the door open. Except that in spite of all his shaking and quaking, he could not manage to collapse either but had to remain standing in front of the locked door, fumbling with his fifty-two keys, fumbling into the evening, fumbling through the night. Now and then he was granted a merciful break that let him lean his head on the door for a long second. But then: 'Back to work! You have no choice!' and before he resumed his desperate fumbling, his head drooping and swaying, a whimper burst out of him, not that of a human but of an animal—an unknown animal. Or he, the other man, thought he heard this? It was out of the question to offer help. The man would come at him with the bunch of keys and would then take off running, down the street, looking for people he could kill: he would run amok. (In the slapstick version of the story the actor had read that morning, all it took to make the protagonist run amok, after his futile attempts to pick up the lemon seed in the house, was a shoelace with a knot that refused to come undone out on the street and a cough-drop wrapping whose loose end he could not find, no matter how hard he tried.)

For a long time, all the small houses and gardens in this last stretch of outskirts on the approach to the city had presented themselves as deserted, many of them also uninhabited, and not merely now for the summer, with a 'For Sale' sign outside every second house. So it gave him confidence that he was going in the right direction when more and more he heard voices and noises behind the hedges and between the houses. Except that these were hardly ever peaceable. What predominated was yelling and uproar—no need to strain one's ears.

The time in which the story of the Great Fall takes place was also a time of wars large and small. The large ones were being waged, with no end in sight, in what we Westerners call third countries, but the small ones were taking place right here in our midst, day out, night in, deadly in different way but also with no end in sight. Civil wars? Nonsense: those seemed, at least hereabouts, to have run their course, and if they flared up again, they would not be small but, rather, the largest or most cruel ones, as civil wars have always been. No, in each country, it was a period of wars between neighbours, a misleading expression because each case involved only two people going at each other while their families, if they had families—a rarity—steered clear of the hostilities. Nonetheless, these were wars fully deserving of the name. In contrast to the large wars, at least those of earlier times, no peace treaty was conceivable. The war between neighbours could end only with the death, a violent one of some kind or other, of one combatant or both. Words were out of the question, and when the shouting stopped that could mean but one thing: the lethal outcome for one or both was near.

The newspapers had special columns devoted to these wars and they grew longer every day. The pretexts for these wars: none, neither noise nor a different language nor skin colour nor religion, not even the possible initial factor of being unable to stand one another. Usually the warring parties were people of approximately the same age who had similar professions and similar origins, used similar, mostly technical, expressions and, in general, resembled each other in all respects. Social scientists had tried to explain the phenomenon as an outgrowth of the long period of peace in our region, which they thought had had a sort of physical effect, creating a space inside individuals where enormous hatred could build up, hatred of everything and everyone, just waiting to be released, specifically on the neighbour next door; the neighbour one or two houses farther down the street was completely out of consideration and could even be a good friend or card buddy. But these explanations cooked up by the psychophysicists had not gained acceptance. The neighbour wars continued to be seen as inexplicable, not least because of the suddenness and primitive ferocity with which the hostilities broke out. A man stepped out of his garden gate, and his neighbour came at him with his father's or his grandfather's World War sabre. Another backed out of his garage onto the street and was rammed by his neighbour who had been waiting for ages in his own car with the engine running. Another had boiling pitch dumped on him from above, and another, by no means the last mentioned in the daily column, was sitting on his terrace one evening reading the paper when his neighbour broke through the hedge and struck him in the back of the neck with a wooden club, hardly less ferociously than Cain must have attacked his brother Abel.

The actor stumbled on such neighbour-to-neighbour wars everywhere. Except that the hostilities were not directed at the other person. The violence was not initially aimed at him, or not yet, but at his possessions, and the owner was often not present; the attacker unleashed his rage only on the other's property, which served as a proxy, and the perpetrator accompanied his actions with shouted words, not attacking in silence, or not yet. One bashed in the roof of his neighbour's car with an iron rod. Another used a jack hammer to attack a dustbin painted in the colours of the rainbow, the bin identical to his own and all the others on the street, all of which, despite their size, were filled to bursting, as if holding several houses' refuse. One of the perpetrators, bellowing war cries, trampled on a sort of wind rose he had yanked off his neighbour's ridge pole with a lasso. One of them performed a war dance on his neighbour's huge outdoor thermometer. Another climbed a step ladder to pee onto his enemy's zucchini plants. Another jumped up and down on the property line and shattered his enemy's air by lashing it with a whip, louder than any whip in a circus. Another lit a fire close to the front line, using God only knows what debris, and blew the stinking smoke in his enemy's direction with one of those infernal machines usually used to blow leaves on the street and not only there, who knows why, along with dust and all sorts of filth, and spread it around. It was an end of days. But people had become accustomed to it. It would never end.

With one of these people overcome by murderous glee, and it was not the last of them, our actor came within a hair's breadth of intervening. He was tempted to snatch the hatchet with whose blunt end the man was hacking at his neighbour's grill—he had the same model in his own garden—out of his hand and split his head with the sharp end, down to his screeching throat! Fortunately, before he did so—'now I'm going for it!'—at the last moment he remembered a scene from the script about the man who runs amok, not slapstick at all, and, without fully realizing how fortunate he was, he continued towards the city.

How the sky shone blue, and how the summer wind blew, and how heart-warmingly sun and shadow played over the shrubs in the gardens, and how the omnipresent God or his oracle spoke in the rustling of the trees and the whispering of the air, and spoke, and spoke: 'Be peaceful, brothers, children, creatures: looking up and listening, turning inward and turning back, and returning—simply being alive is a blessing,' yet none of the destroyers listened or thought for a moment of looking up and listening, each one convinced he had justice on his side in his world war, even seeing himself as pleasing to God, indeed carrying out God's will. The words of God or his oracle would fade away, or had they already faded away? Since when? Since the genocides? Since the atom bombs on Hiroshima and Nagasaki? Or since way back with the millions of casualties from the First World War? Or even earlier? And along with God's words, Heaven and Earth would fade away, or had long since faded away, and the earth had ceased to be God's world as well as mankind's. 'I should have bashed in the skulls of every one of them,' he said out loud to himself, 'made their brains squirt out of their dead eyes and ears, broken their necks with a chop of my hand, sent them to hell with a flame-thrower—if only hell existed—and all the filming tomorrow would be unnecessary . . . ' Sometimes he thought of himself as born to be a misanthrope, precisely as an actor, especially at times when he was between jobs. Or, to put it differently, between jobs, he was more of an actor than ever, ready for anything or nothing.

Without warning, he found himself on the verge of intervening, or at least getting involved.

Instead, he broke into a run, away from the battle-fields, a slow run, in the course of which he tried to become conscious of each part of his body, more or less in the spirit of the maxim 'The whole man must move at once,' and to connect all the parts, a run he called the Gentle Run, in memory of a film made many decades ago. For quite a while now, the moment had come almost daily when he felt compelled to run, for short stretches only, sometimes just a few steps. 'It's time for the Gentle Run,' he told himself. On the day of the Great Fall, the time for the Gentle Run arrived earlier than ever before. And the run did not have the effects that its name alone usually guaranteed. And what had those effects been? The Gentle Run had surveyed his surroundings for him, dividing them into circles, triangles, squares, trapezoids, parallel-ograms, in the sense of the old saying: 'The deity is constantly surveying the earth.' The deity was always geometricizing? The gentle runners as geometers? As earth-circlers? Or, to put it differently again, the Gentle Run was not only the carpenter's level but also the air-, fire- and earth-scales, the ele-mental scales? The elemental measure?

Suddenly, the actor began to feel hunger as he ran. It was his second hunger of the day, and the first true one. It was a hunger for food, and a hunger for more, much more. The hunger became so great that he, as the hungry one, no, the hungering one, felt close to tears. Soon he would begin to cry, no, burst out sobbing, and never be able to stop. No, he would neither cry nor sob; rather, if his hunger were not slaked soon, he would die on the spot. His hunger for food was intensified by his hunger for a woman, no, for the woman down there in the heart of the city—to unite with her now, now, not like the animal but like the god with two backs—and his hunger for the woman was intensified by his hunger for—yes, for what? What could it be? And finally it came to him. As little use as the actor had for the Goethe responsible for Faust, he cherished the other Goethe's inspiring notion of the 'higher power', meaning the spirit. Yes, it was hunger for food, for the woman and for the spirit, all rolled up in one, that he felt pounding inside him. There, on the spot, he would die if he did not come upon the spirit very soon. 'Veni, creator spiritus!'

If he now kept his eyes peeled for a house of God, he was merely responding to his mortal fear, guided by nothing but instinct. For some time now, amid all the racket and rumpus, a bell had made itself heard, not a tolling or summoning but just a single clang at intervals of several long seconds. No particular hour was being struck. The repeated clang, always the same, that seemingly refused to end, was in a minor key, or perhaps that was how it reached the eardrum. Although rather quiet, once noticed, it drowned out the uproar down on earth and aloft, also the roaring and honking from the the city beltway he was approaching. The bell's one note had an overwhelming and increasingly pervasive sadness to it. It could not be a cemetery bell, for this was no tolling for a funeral and certainly no jangling death knell such as he had once set in motion himself, right after the death of his father, when he dashed in the cold grey light of dawn to the church, once the death rattle had ceased, and tugged on the thinnest bell rope there, with only one hand—that was how small it was, the death bell. The one he was hearing now must be a full-sized bell. And not being rung by a person; the clapper struck automatically against the cast iron or whatever; as far as he was concerned, it could also be a gong, and the bell was a temple bell. Or it was three o'clock in the afternoon and the tolling of the bell was meant to invoke the death on the Cross at Golgotha? He did not want to know and forced himself not to check the time.

He had time, 'still', and so it happened that he followed the sound of the bell—it came, 'I'm certain, for a change,' from a house of God, whether a church, temple or mosque. It was a church, as small as the houses along the street, recognizable only by its small tower, the blue paint faded, and by a rusty cross on top that could just as well be a television antenna. At once his fear subsided and his run became gentle—one that was soothing to him and to any people he might encounter. (There were none.) And in his searing hunger for a certain body and likewise for the creator spirit, he could predict one thing: the house of God would be open and, in spite of the afternoon hour, a Mass would be under way, and he would arrive at just the right moment.

And so it was. The candles on the altar had just been lit and the priest in full regalia was already seated in the open sacristy preparing for the service, engrossed in his book and, at the same time, completely alert. The actor was the only one in the spacious nave and remained so during the service. The priest at the altar moved his lips without a sound, reading a silent Mass, as it had been known in the past or was still known. The sole visitor associated such a silent Mass more with early morning, as the first Mass of the day, taking place long before any others, just as long ago, when he rang the death knell for his father in the church located in the land of the ancient river, a silent Mass had been taking place, or did he only imagine that?

It was perfectly fine that, from the Kyrie Eleison to the reading of the Epistles and then the Gospel from the altar, nothing could be heard in the nave but occasional sounds from the priest's lips as he ran through the familiar words; also fine that the visitor seemed invisible to the cleric, as if he were conducting the service entirely for himself, and as if the occasional sign of the cross that he made silently as he turned to face the nave were intended equally for the one moth there, for the dust swirling in a ray of sun, the empty swallow's nest below the choir loft and, above all, for the empty space itself.

During the ceremony, the monotonous gong or bell continued to clang, on the same note but now without the overtone of sorrow. It was after the Gospel reading that the priest turned again and, without imparting a blessing to anyone, raised himself to his full height, acquiring in his gold-embroidered robes the stature of a giant, and speaking loudly, delivered what sounded like a sermon, an urgent one, which, had no one else been present, he would have addressed to the dust in the cone of sunlight, to the wood worms in the pews, to himself. And yet what he said was meant for the other person, although the priest looked past him while speaking, meant specifically for him, as if the priest had been reading his thoughts while reading the Mass: 'Yes, God's impotence! But His omnipresence is His strength, His only might, or would be, if. It would be a strength, and what a strength, if I, when I needed it, could become cognisant of it and turn to it. And I do need it. But where should I turn? And how? And, yes! The woman's body represents the earthly manifestation of the spirit's omnipresence during the night. Together with the woman a new language comes into play, a different sound makes itself heard. And may this continue, on and on! All hail to bodies. The woman, the different letter of the alphabet. It's not I who take the woman but the woman who takes me, and my flesh becomes spirit. I, the hungering man, she, the thirsting woman—the man of hunger, the woman of thirst! Desire for desire of the other! Nothing means more than desire, than the hunger and thirst we both feel. Raise up both our hearts. Amen. So it is. So be it.'

During the transubstantiation of the bread into the body and the wine into the blood, it would have been appropriate for the sole communicant to fall to his knees. That was something the actor had never succeeded in doing, even in films, and now, too, he merely flexed his knees in his pew, as he had done since childhood, counting on the priest's recognizing that as kneeling. But at the same moment he felt a need, a yearning—or was it part of his hunger?—not just to fall to his knees but to prostrate himself and remain lying face down, and, at the same time, it was a relief that there was no way he could hurl himself to the ground between the pews. He skipped Communion; the priest was left alone at the altar to consume the host. He took a second one from the chalice and held it up invitingly, then laid it back in the chalice. The final blessing, 'Go in peace,' the priest formulated in the informal second person singular, turning to the one man there: 'Go in peace!'

After that the actor was invited into the sacristy for a meal. The priest removed his robes, and underneath he was wearing blue workman's garb that his guest found confidence-inspiring. The serenity with which the celebration of the Eucharist had filled him persisted, and everything transformed by the ceremony into what it was—a table, spiderwebs—was enhanced by the victuals, including a bottle of wine which the priest produced from a plastic supermarket bag, along with a couple of paper plates. The table, which moments earlier had served as a place to lay the gold-embroidered robes, became a dining table. Curious the way eating could make one reflective, or how, conversely, a certain reflectiveness could make the most ordinary food tasty, and how one felt protected during such eating and wanted it to go on and on.

The priest's exclamation, directed at no one in particular: 'How one loses one's taste for food when one eats alone! Even the best food lacks flavour. But a meal like the one we've just had, no matter what it consists of—how delicious.' And he began to talk. His vocation had come to him late, after a life spent as an auto mechanic; and following the meal, he intended to go out to the garden behind the church and pick the first apples, early apples; before being incorporated into the city, this area had had extensive orchards belonging to the Crown, with rare kinds of fruit, royal varieties, in fact. The serenity they both felt stayed with them after the meal when they tidied up the sacristy together and made some repairs, and it would not wane all that soon. It seemed entirely natural that the stranger had various small tools with him—a screwdriver, sandpaper, scissors—and willingly lent a hand. And when he finally fished sewing needles and silver and gold thread out of a kit in an inner jacket pocket and set to work mending one of the priest's robes, the priest tried to guess his profession. In spite of his elegant suit and his necktie, the priest surmised, the other man was not a distinguished gentleman, not a gentleman at all. One look at his hands revealed that he was accustomed to working with them; that from a young age, he had pitched in. Upon entering the church, before he removed his narrow-brimmed hat with the two falcon feathers, he, the priest, had taken him for a king, a Louis, no, not the Sun King but a Louis from several centuries earlier, the one who had been crowned while he was still a child and, as a solemn adult king, had remained a child all his life and had come to be called Saint Louis, because of the Crusades (on one of which he died), or in spite of these Crusades, which were actually rather childish, and not merely from today's perspective, and in the priest's eyes was therefore a saint nonetheless, such as only Francis of Assisi was, and a royal miraculous healer. Or maybe the other man was a desperado, an outlaw. There was something violent about him. True, he had not yet killed anyone, but he seemed capable of it, would kill some day, perhaps this very day. Or he was a nobody and that seemed to the priest the most likely explanation, no one special, a scarecrow in the middle of a field whose appearance changed according to the wind and the light, one moment a giant, a bundle of misery the next, looking now like a woman, now like a couple, now like an entire tribe and, finally, like no one and nothing at all. But whatever the case, the other man came from a third country and he was welcome here. And the priest then gave the actor a first name: 'Christopher—for you bear on your shoulders the weight of the world! And it's fitting that you have an expression around your mouth of one who has drunk life's bitterness almost to the dregs, and not even unwillingly.'

Then the other man took his turn guessing about the priest, keeping his eye on a painting on the wall of the sacristy that showed a man at a standing desk, writing with his right hand and pressing a half-hidden object to his lips with the left: that must be the glowing ember with which the prophet kept himself alert while transcribing his visions? A good guess, or maybe not: for he, the priest, saw the thing the writer was using to keep himself in line not as a burning ember but as a ball of clay, or even more likely a fresh snowball, a particularly icy one, and it was pressed to his lips, and likewise the writer's lips pressed themselves to it. Finally, the priest returned to his guessing: 'But all joking aside, you're neither a king nor a desperado, Brother Christopher. You're an actor. How did I know? It's your unobtrusiveness, your "nonperson" manner. Even alone on a wide plain you could be overlooked. And what else gave you away? Your complete seriousness, your air of inward and outward concentration. And what else gave you away? Your straightforwardness, your lack of affectation. Your scrupulousness. And why did I recognize all that? Because as a priest, I'm a kind of actor, too, I have to be.'

The actor continued his pilgrimage towards the city with a spring in his step and the joy he felt was different from most of the joys of recent years. 'So what were those joys like?' (Talking to himself.) 'First of all, they did not come along very often. And then they were over soon. They broke off abruptly or I broke them off myself. And that happened because when my joy wanted to expand beyond me, the moment inevitably came when it collided with others' unhappiness, with my awareness of others' suffering and desolation. It did no good to stop reading the papers and watching TV. It was not just the constant awareness of tsunami victims, famines, wars in the second and innumerable other worlds. I had only to think of my son, far away and alone—even if I merely pictured him that way—and I would feel unentitled to any joy. And yet it was precisely when I was joyful that I had the clearest sense of being able to imagine, be aware of, empathize with another person. My joy, at its outer limit, was joined by an urge to help, and when there was no way to help, my joy broke off. My joy became impermissible. And eventually, it ceased altogether. And yet, it existed, had to exist, for I had experienced it. Except that I no longer knew what it was.'

His joy on this day, the day of the Great Fall, remained untarnished by the unhappiness of others. Or no: unhappiness became omnipresent, as part of his joy, permeating it instead of cancelling it out. It was a joy laced with pain that accompanied his pilgrimage, and in it, with it and through it, he experienced no sense of being in the wrong and no guilty conscience—it was not personal joy that bore him along, and it had nothing to do with him as an individual; it transcended him. This painful joy was unanimous. He shared it, even though he was walking along all by himself, shared

it with whom? With no one and nothing in particular, with the summery air, the horizons, the dog
excrement in the gutter, with a parking permit and
a receipt from a chemist's that someone had discarded. And this joy would not have come to him
from standing alone in the empty church or from
any other form of solitude. It came from a catharsis, the result of the ceremony he had shared—
never mind that there had been only two of
them—and the catharsis might have resulted just
as well from a ceremony other than a Mass?
Maybe, but maybe not. This shared joy was not
something he had fallen into. How beautifully it
hurt. How his trouser legs flapped like sails as he
walked. How much energy that generated. For
doing something? For leaving something undone.
Yes, it was decided: the actor would not attend the
celebration being held in his honour that evening
down in the capital. And the shoot the following
morning?

He hesitated again when, shortly before he
reached the beltway, he came upon a street that
stretched straight ahead into the undulating
distance, with hardly any houses, with strips of
crushed rock on either side, a street that resembled
a cross-country highway and to which he involuntarily said, 'Salve, Carretera, Magistrala, Highway

66!' Should he work his way back on this road, away from the city?

He forgot that thought the moment a bus came towards him from the city, a very tall, steel-blue, brand-new bus, packed with soldiers on their way to their barracks, but at the wheel, standing out from the others, a person as civilian as one could possibly be: a young woman with long, flowing blond hair, a woman of a beauty impossible to miss, and this beauty waved to him as he stood on the shoulder of the Carretera, her eyes wide, without smiling, her face completely serious. Or had she waved to someone else, in a car behind him? No car had come towards the bus and there were no other pedestrians on the road.

SEVEN

Into the city—what choice did he have? He walked like an Indian in a John Ford film whose name, in his native language, Navajo, described a certain gait, and he had noted this description and often repeated it to himself in particular situations: 'Haske Yichi Nixwod', which meant more or less 'he who walks resolutely'.

On the balcony of one of the increasingly numerous houses lining the road, which soon was no longer a 'highway', sat a very old lady, with her snow-white hair loose like that of the woman bus driver and an equally serious expression, who blew him a kiss when he looked up and greeted her. And by the embankment before the beltway, where the road ended, an even older lady stood in the wind, flying a kite, and, when it crashed onto the pavement, she gave the man approaching a grin reminiscent of bygone times. Before that, he had finally come upon a shop by the roadside, a shop that resembled a trading post, likewise from bygone times, and there he had of course become a customer, purchasing various small items. These things, too, money and merchandise, demand and supply, buying and selling were in accord with the impersonal serenity of the hour. The newspapers in that shop had not found a single buyer up to then. None had been sold yesterday either and, according to the proprietor, 'just one' the previous day. And the Magistrale had been spared the neighbour-wars, or had he merely failed to see and hear them? The sign outside the shop, its lettering very faded, said nothing but ULTRAMARINOS, overseas products, and inside, on an étagère, single items—one papaya, one pineapple, one blackish banana and one (1) very black piece of monkey bread, which he also purchased and ate as he continued on his way, as he had long ago in childhood, and it also tasted the way it had back then and, at the same time, completely different.

The embankment that marked the end of the outer districts was an earthen berm, on the other side of which the beltway was located in a cut. The beltway also produced a kind of ringing, constant, unceasing, seemingly coming from underground. The actor could have taken one of the walking and biking paths along the berm; somewhere an overpass or a tunnel had to lead to the other side of the beltway. Instead, he scrambled up the embankment, facing backwards again, as he had left the forest. Climbing backwards—was that possible?

And walking backwards resolutely? Ah, the special sound feet made when going backwards, a sound evocative of the here-and-now if ever there was one, such a fresh new sound! A sound of knocking, knocking on the door to the here-and-now. And he pictured a film with the title *The New Here-and-Now*.

Having reached the crest of the embankment, he turned to face in the direction in which he planned to go and forced his way through a tangle of thorny shrubbery. Crouching in the bushes was an entire family of hares. They merely went through the motions of hopping away when he slipped through, perhaps because he saluted them, his palm slightly raised. Single hares, each at the entry to its burrow, also occupied the other side of the embankment, which was grassy and sloped steeply to the highway far below, and, along with the hares, ravens, as if an essential feature of summer, and a single fox lying quietly by its lair, and a couple of feral dogs, which, it seemed, were not all that feral. The traffic below rushed along with a roaring and braying that did not let up for a single moment, let alone break off. Groping his way down the steep bank, slowly, one step at a time, with the feral dogs wagging their tails at him and barking unusually softly, if at all, consistent with the fact that in his films, the actor never raised his voice, and when one would have expected him to shout, lowered his voice even more—again not a technique; he was simply incapable of shouting. Amid the braying and roaring, fragments of a song burst through an open car window: ' . . . a wonderful night for a moon dance!' And then a long, long interval of honking for a newlywed couple. Yes, does such a thing happen? Yes, did such a thing still happen?

He would cross the expressway on foot, and that was no bet this time. No need to describe the successful crossing, which he executed at a moment for which he had waited a long time and which he had been certain would come, and the same with the second moment, after an even longer wait, if possible, on the median strip. Don't ask me how he made it to the embankment on the other side. He ran, and as he broke into a run, he already knew that nothing would happen to him, or to the cars, which honked at him as expected but did not need to brake to avoid him. Once arrived on the other shore, he did not pause but began scrambling up the slope—anything to avoid looking back—where other hares, ravens and dogs stood at attention.

Atop the embankment, it was still not the city's inner quarters that awaited him. Creeping rather than crawling through thorny underbrush again, and not on his stomach but on his back, feet first, because they were best at clearing a path. And once through there and out in the open, when he stood up, he saw before him only a rail yard, but one that stretched to the horizon, and on the horizon another barrier of underbrush, no, something taller, perhaps a small forest—not visible from higher up—and the train tracks running towards the horizons to the left and right seemed to lead into the void, with no glimpse of the towers of the metropolis. The rail yard itself was completely deserted, except for what must have been hundreds of rusty rails and equally rusty and twisted switches poking up from them. Tall grass and thistles grew luxuriantly between the remaining cross ties and covered all the crushed rock except for a few light patches. He stood there, surveying a far-flung swath of no-man's-land such as one found only in metropolises, the very largest ones, and often close to their centres, which from the countryside remained invisible and, amazingly, almost inaudible, a phenomenon that was not all that unusual.

He made his way through the no-man's-land in wide loops. He 'still' had time, still. Although there was hardly anything to see there, it was as if one could not look one's fill. It was unacceptable to ignore a single rail; one had to measure off, with longer or shorter paces, the varying gaps between the ties; the absolute nothingness, where there had once been something and would be again some day, demanded to be accounted for, along with the great sky, arching overhead as it hardly did anywhere else these days.

In the midst of his no-man's-land, he heard from the other side, from the forest or city side, someone whistle, and it was immediately clear that it was meant for him, the vagrant in the rail yard. Some one had whistled at him, not with a metal whistle but with two fingers, and how. On the far side, a car had driven up and two men had jumped out. Now they stood there, legs splayed as far apart as was humanly possible, and one of them waved him over while the other whistled at him, again fitting because the actor never whistled in his films, or at least not that way, at most between his teeth, and in that case in the rhythm of a melody. This whistling had no melody, as indeed the summoning, accomplished with an index finger, was not appealing.

'Your way of summoning is not appealing,' the actor said when he reached the two men. In response, the whistler patted once, then again, the gun holster on his hip, from which the object for which it was designed protruded, impossible to miss. 'Police!' Unspoken question: What, not in uniform, in plain clothes, and with a car that could just as well be stolen, without identifying markings? And the answer again: two taps on a band, frayed and filthy, around his upper arm, on which the word 'police' could be read in the language of the country, although one or two of the letters had to be guessed at.

He had wandered into a prohibited area; the former rail yard was off limits. Had he overlooked the no-entry sign and the barrier on the access road? How had he got in? Cut the barbed wire? He had a foreign accent, from a hostile country, or hostile at one time, even if that had been centuries ago. Enmities between peoples lasted, lasted a long time and could flare up again today or tomorrow, *n'est-ce pas*? What was he doing here? There was nothing in this area, nothing to see, no historical monument and certainly no cultural heritage site. Didn't he have anything better to do? Why did he seem to have time, all the time in the world? That alone was suspicious. And why time for this desert here? He had heard right: 'desert' had always been the local expression for any empty stretch, even if it had springs bubbling up and green grass, and, amid all the green, fruits of various kinds. But no such thing in the dead rail yard. So? 'What act of violence are you staging from here? Admit it: you're an assassin. You're preparing a murderous attack, possibly on our head of state. He keeps receiving death threats, in letters written in bad grammar, like yours. Empty your pockets, and make it snappy!'

When he did not comply quickly enough, one of the two agents reached out and in no time had turned all his suit pockets inside out, including those on the inside and in the back, as well as the slit pocket, with the result that everything he had on him lay strewn on the ground, still muddy from the morning's storm. In roughing him up, the policeman had casually knocked off the hat with the falcon feathers, and he twisted the actor's arm behind his back with the words, 'Adhesive tape, screws, keys, matches, fuse timer disguised as a mobile phone, penknife that pretends to be little but plays the field—saw, scissors, reamer, tweezers and pocket torch all in one. If that's not conclusive evidence. Confess, you pathetic lone wolf. Don't you know that no lone wolf ever achieved what he set out to do? That Rastignac didn't act alone and neither did Gavrilo Princip or Lee Harvey Oswald?'

Meanwhile the second policeman bent down, picked up the objects and stuffed them into the actor's pockets again after carefully pushing them back in place. Then he moved aside, whereupon his partner let go of the actor's twisted arm—but left it where it was, behind his back—and stared at the would-be violent perpetrator for a second so intently that the actor felt as if he were staring at himself. Then the second policeman, or whatever he was (approximately as old, or as young, as the first one, by the way), said, 'I hope you didn't come here to do yourself harm? To take your life? You should know, monsieur, dear sir'—and this he said in the actor's mother-and-father tongue— 'that this area attracts suicides. That's another reason we patrol here.' The first man, interrupting him: 'Don't you dare do yourself in here and leave us a stinking cadaver to clean up. This is a public place, no suicides allowed. And besides, this isn't your country. Go back to your own country if you're going to kick the bucket!' But then the second policeman did not allow himself to be interrupted and continued more or less as follows, still staring intently at the actor: 'My partner means

what he says, that's how he is, that's how he was
when we were assigned to each other and he's not
going to change. And you, sir, monsieur, signore,
caballero, will go in peace now, even though it's
plain as day that you're a threat, whether to others
or yourself I don't know. No, not a threat, it's less
than that and more. Good luck to you, here and
elsewhere! Today alone, twenty-one people in this
region have already jumped in front of trains or
been pushed.' And he shook the hand of the actor,
who replied, 'But no trains are running here,'
whereupon the two policemen climbed into their
car, whose engine had been left idling the entire
time and, before he knew it, they had disappeared
into the little jungle bordering the rail yard.

It was a jungle, though a narrow one, a mere
strip between the rail yard and the ocean of a city
down below. This became apparent as he entered
it, not on the unpaved track, muddy, with puddles
seemingly left over from the last rainy season, on
which the police car, or whatever it was, had sped
out of sight in classic film fashion. Entering this
jungle was no picnic; he had to fight his way
through, and that was what he wanted, what had
to happen now. No one else would have got
through such a thicket, the undergrowth more tangled than any fence woven of willow shoots. But

he anticipated every step, skirting obstacles, rolling himself into a ball, making himself skinny or wide, and he was also certain that he would make it to the other side and how he would do it, as one sometimes knows when winding up to throw something that it will hit the target. And this time he did not even tear his clothing, which—I forgot to mention this—had been mended earlier at the table in the sacristy, along with the priest's robes. The words spoken by the second policeman had planted an idea in his mind and he wanted to get it out of his head while crossing the jungle. He was reminded of his father—he, too, had always hurled words at him that had never occurred to him before. And they were never words that helped or provided insight but, rather, words that diminished him, hemmed him in, words that expressed nothing but pessimism about the son's prospects. And yet that policeman had been younger, much younger than he, could have been his son.

On the far side of the jungle, he suddenly found himself surrounded by the city and, for a moment, he thought he was on a hill that included the heart of the metropolis. At any rate, he was standing atop a steep incline, and it seemed as if even the tallest buildings along the horizons barely rose to that altitude, and as if the ground on which the city below rested were so far down that if he took one more step, he would hurtle into thin air. And why not, after all—onward!—at which he remembered how sometimes, when he was young, whether drunk or not, and found himself at a dizzying height, on the terrace of a television tower, for instance, he had toyed with the idea of letting himself fall, silently, just as a thought experiment and not really meaning it. But one time, he put it into words, in the company of a woman: 'Now I'm going to jump!' and then felt he had to make good on his threat but, in the end, let the woman hold him back, without any fuss and gratefully.

Now there was no real danger, and not only because the abyss turned out to be an optical illusion—once he had taken the first step after breaking through the thicket, it revealed itself as such. He resolved to refrain from invoking the magnetic attraction of the depths, even to himself. Instead, he lay down quietly in the manicured grass of the steep slope—which belonged a strip or ring of parkland, similar to the beltway from earlier, and the ring of parkland belonged to the city centre, as did everything as far as the eye could see, and it could see farther than far: the church towers, minarets, banks, telephone and TV hubs, the river with its series of bridges as well as the gardens in-between, the allotment colonies, the market stalls, the bus shelters and even the individual trees, the tram tracks, the Metro entrances, the traffic lights there, and over there, and certainly the baby carriage, the dustbin, the hydrant, the public toilet—all belonged to the centre.

He stretched out and gazed up at the sky. Why did that other actor come to mind, one of his few friends, and someone with the same profession, no less? One evening or one night, the other man had lain down in the sand between the land of the ancient river and the North Sea mudflats and had let the tide wash him away from his earthly life. He had been a heavy man but light on his feet. The actor lying there, on the other hand, would not have been heavy enough, not yet, not now. Besides, he was in no mood to die, at most to fade away and yet survive. And perhaps that was what his friend had been hoping for, too, as he lay there on the border between life and death? And what was he hoping for now? A bird, for instance, that would defecate on him out of the clear blue sky, right here, in the middle of my forehead, be my guest. And then a lump of bird dropping actually plopped onto the grass next to him, missing him, alas.

A single little white cloud puffed itself up in the sun-drenched blue sky, took on colours, transparent ones, fairy-tale colours, and developed something resembling a head, and flapped its wings, or perhaps a delicate voluminous garment. A rose unfurling? No, a jellyfish that oozed across the sky towards him, swelling and shrinking and swelling again. And the long, loose spider's thread that blew just above him out of the thicket widened and contracted, then curled, took on a silvery sheen, displayed a pattern of diamond shapes and then tickled him with its tip, in the form of a snakeskin, as soft and tender as could be imagined, that, too, part of the city centre, constituting the centre.

His eyes fell shut and, try though he would to open them, he did not succeed. As he lay there on the grassy slope, his feet stretching into what could have been an abyss but was not, he sensed danger, though not for himself. He felt newly enveloped by the summer wind, blowing steadily, an upwind in relation to where he was lying, coming from each of the centres below, and the sounds of the metropolis, even and sonorous, wrapped him from all sides and also protected him.

The danger threatened someone else, his son, to be specific. Yet his son was already a young man and could take care of himself, no? And if he needed help, it would be better coming from someone else. Wasn't he surrounded by others like him who over time had become his real relatives and would be there to help in an emergency? His long-absent father had lost his right to be his helper and would have been no help in any case; more help was to be had from his deceased mother.

But it was not a question of help. Of what, then? Of salvation. And for saving him, he, the father, was indeed the right person, that much was certain. It was up to him. But how to save his son? And from what threat? From what situation? It was not that the young man was adrift in water, being swept towards rapids, at Niagara Falls, for instance, or that he was lying unnoticed in the underbrush, seriously injured after an accident, or that he had fallen into a nest of vipers while hiking alone on the southern slope of a mountain range in the karst. He saw his son in mortal danger, acute danger, but not from anything external. He saw that without him the child would be done for, within the hour. He saw his own flesh and blood—never before had he felt himself to be that to his offspring!—sprout a third hand from inside his chest, a clenched fist, and that would be his undoing. And he saw himself break into a run and cross rivers and mountains in a single hour to get to him. And he saw him reach the boy in the nick of time, the way it happens in films. And save him.

But—that question again—how? For there was nothing to save—was there?—from an internal danger like that, from a third hand that turned against its owner. He saved him, forced the clenched fist inside his son to disappear, rendered it weightless and insubstantial by sacrificing himself, right, sacrificing. Sacrificing himself like Eastwood in his last, or next-to-last, or next-to-next-to-last film, in which he, as an old man, let himself to be shot to bring peace to a community mired in mortal conflict? No, not like Clint. He would not sacrifice himself for peace and for a community, or the community of humankind. True, he would put his whole life on the line, and not merely by playing a role; he would know he had to die in the attempt. But he would sacrifice himself solely for his son, for nothing and no one else, not for the woman and not for a neighbour, or a stranger, not even for world peace.

The son's dire situation, together with the father's willingness to sacrifice himself, was so tangible that my actor, when he finally managed to open his eyes, leapt to his feet as if to keep running towards the emergency. If he had been dreaming, it had been, as had happened only a couple of times, far too seldom, an actual situation—a situation that had been predicted. According to the prediction, it was time for him to set out to sacrifice himself. And at the same time it seemed—almost—equally real to him that, during the time when he could not for the life of him open his eyes, his shoes, which he had taken off for his rest and placed beside him in the grass, had disappeared, been stolen, and that that meant he could not go on, could not go anywhere, had to remain on this very spot till the cows came home. Suddenly an understandable wish: if he had to die, at least 'with my shoes on'.

But there they stood, his shoes, not even all that dirty or dusty, despite his having walked in them almost all day, and as if made for continuing on. And at this point, the actor had to come to grips with a dire situation of his own. It was a dire situation that befell him once a day: being short of time. Just a little while ago he had had time, and suddenly he had none.

On the day of the Great Fall, this lack of time came out of the clear blue sky. He had had time before, and expected to have all the time in the world once he had made the decision to skip the evening's event. He was even playing with the idea of leaving the woman in the city to her own devices, and now, contrary to expectation, he had run out of time. Was that because of the change in the light, from which the summery glow had disappeared during the hour when his eyes had been closed, and which, although still clear and showing all contours distinctly, if possible even clearer than before, would no longer have been sufficient for daytime scenes in a film—did this come from the 'broken light'?

Being short of time meant chaos. It was chaos in every respect, in time as in space, in body and soul, in himself and his relations with others. On a film set, competent as he was, he could have opened a door with one hand and simultaneously given the 'dead man' a kick, while speaking one of the complicated sentences that occurred in all his parts, sentences that often had no bearing on the scene at hand and had been contributed to the script by none other than him.

During that late-afternoon hour, however, having awoken in the midst of the city and high above it—if indeed he had actually slept—he became helplessly tangled in his shortage of time, put his shoes on the wrong feet and squashed his hat onto his head inside out with the lining showing. While picking up the book he had used as a pillow, he ripped out the page to which it was open, and he twisted the frame of his sunglasses, which he put on as if all of a sudden he needed a disguise, after going through the entire day completely open and undisguised. And would the glasses with the cockeyed lenses, one of them halfway up his forehead and the other halfway down his cheek, do the trick? His wish: that the two policemen would come back and arrest him, to protect him from himself, among other things.

Dearth of time, time of dearth: without being in a hurry, one had to hurry. Up became down, right became left, in front became in back, ahead became behind and vice versa, and so forth in crazy confusion. The smallest houses towered above him, the river flowed upstream, then briefly downstream again, and next in God only knows what direction, and the passers-by on the street: Were they moving towards him? Away from him? Impossible to tell with the sun so low in the sky. And what else did the shortage of time mean? One became confused about time itself. Was it morning or evening? No idea what day or what year it was. And in general, no idea one could get a grip on, neither a where, a when, certainly not a who, a person. If any thinking at all, then only in numbers, and nonsensical ones, consistent with the lack of time, and could one really call that thinking? And all accompanied by a kind of toneless humming inside one, interminable, starting up again and again and making the confusion total. A humming of something specific, with an identifiable text? Yes, the Ode to Joy. 'Joy, thou lovely spark divine, daughter from Elysium . . . '

In hours when time was desperately needed and the desperation acute, it had happened repeatedly that my actor had stopped moving at the height of the confusion and said to himself, 'It's over. I'm going to drop everything. From now on I won't lift a finger. Not another word. The black cloud on the horizon has come over me—it is me myself. The evil moon has risen—it is me myself. Stay away from me, all of you, now and in the hour of my death, which is now.' That was how he had spoken to himself on that morning many years ago when he had set out to lay a tile floor in a villa on a North Sea island and had paused, deciding to abandon that line of work, once and for all. And who had saved him that time? A woman, one who had been dead now for a long time, whose words would echo in his ears until his own end—they were spoken into a telephone in the transcontinental hospital in Fairbanks, Alaska, and they were her last: 'I'm so tired.' Or less those three little dying words than her voice. What a voice. So had he, intent on being a saviour, been saved himself, at least on that occasion? Yes, by a woman, by an adventurer, as his woman had been. And when he thought of his own salvation, did he still think of being saved by a woman? Was he even thinking of salvation now? Did he even want to be saved? No reply. What got him moving again, with time so short, was the tried-and-true thought of being his own audience, rather as a drunk runs into someone completely hammered and as a result almost becomes sober himself.

The process of becoming sober finally made it possible for him to reflect on the lack of time. That lack had been accompanied by a monstrous sense of boredom, and the boredom had gone hand in hand with a hectic sense of urgency, and most of all an inability to pay attention. With time in such short supply the earth was not merely an alien planet but a hostile one as well. And how strange that this lack manifested itself only on days of leisure. But wasn't having leisure a necessity? And therefore also running out of time?

EIGHT

On the day of the Great Fall, he left nothing, nothing at all, behind. He gathered up his possessions as best he could and hurtled down the steep slope, once part of a medieval rampart and, unlike the grassy mound up above, apparently excavated quite recently, its stones laid bare, looking almost polished. It was an actual hurtling, and the way he stumbled downhill headfirst he could have fallen to his death, and not only because of his loose shoelaces. 'I'm sure I have a guardian angel, or several, actually. And in the course of my life I've already used up some of them. And at some point I will have used up all of them.'

Down below, having reached the threshold of the inner city, the actor would have been able to take a few steps backwards again, as he usually did when leaving a place. But there could be no question of that now. He would not go backwards any more from now to the end of his story, not look back over his shoulder, and also not take any detours, but would rather go straight ahead, regardless of whether he deviated from his course time and again. No more King Backwards-Walker.

The threshold to the inner districts was marked by one of the newly installed public toilets. From the outside, this one looked rather small, but it expanded when one entered, not unlike the nave of the church on the outskirts earlier. It became more spacious still, if possible, once one had closed and locked the door behind one. From the cupola subdued light streamed over the azure-blue tiles with which the entire space was laid and which softly reflected the light. He could have laid these tiles himself, leaving openings for the toilet bowls. The solemn organ music that filled the place was actually the constant rushing of water. There was none of that public-toilet smell or any other smell; even the urine had no odour. Nothing but a gentle draft perceptible everywhere, as on the crest of a hill remote from the world. After he had washed up thoroughly and in other respects made himself presentable for the city, he stayed in the facility for a long, long time. At first he turned on the timed light every time it switched off. Then he stayed in the dark. The darkness was total, no crack anywhere through which so much as a glimmer might come from the outside. Should he stay there for ever in the blackness? Disappear in it? Never return to the light? The actor stood motionless and listened. With the water rushing nothing could be heard from the city but fire and police sirens, and even those were as faint as if coming from another planet and another era. And at the same time he felt in every cell that he was in the city and that it was expecting him as intently as it had ever expected anyone. A compulsion to change clothes for it, for the centre, to alter at least one item of his clothing. He turned the back brim of his hat to the front.

Outside another change in the light, not yet that of evening, but the sunlight interwoven with a veil of oncoming darkness. No darker light than sometimes in summertime, the light of a solar eclipse but without the moon or anything else blocking the sun. Long lingering on this spatial and temporal threshold. Walking up and down, functioning again as a geometer. Then out on the street leading into the central districts such an unceasing roar, underlaid with the roar of the parallel streets, that a kind of inaudibility prevailed; no individual sounds could be made out distinctly. At most noticeable the way the young people spoke with the voices of old people, or much older people.

Hardly any older or old people were out and about, that, too, in contrast to the outer or in-between districts. Their absence became even more evident from the glossy placards that lined the streets, advertising high-rise apartment buildings soon to be built: one could see future tenants, looking three-dimensional and true to life, strolling beneath hundreds of balconies dripping with flowers in brilliantly green parks, alone, in couples, with children, and not one of those portrayed was an older or elderly person, let alone one with a cane; not even a middle-aged person was envisaged as a potential buyer. But then on the pavement below these placards appeared an old lady after all, wandering back and forth confusedly between several bus-stop poles, looking for the one bus that would carry her back to the periphery or beyond: in vain, for the young policemen, strangers there themselves, could not help her and had other things to do besides, acting in their official capacity to check the papers of people their own age, for which reason the old lady was asked politely to stay out of the way to allow them, the policemen, to proceed unimpeded. If the actor had looked back from the end of the long street, he would have seen the confused white-haired woman continuing to circle the men in uniform, asking the only clearly audible question in the entire city: 'Excuse me, where is the stop for the bus to . . . ?' Instead, as he walked straight ahead, he looked only to left and right, where the buildings slated for demolition were covered either with paintings or with graffiti, the paintings imitating the sprayed-on graffiti but in colours that were harmonious, as were the figures portrayed, and the situations, scenes and accompanying symbols, words, sentences and exclamations were comprehensible, whereas the graffiti-covered walls were layered with jagged lines like flashes of lightning and exclamations, all in black spray paint and incomprehensible. No doubt they meant something, too, something that graffiti scholars had long since decoded. But the actor felt no desire at all to understand them; the incomprehensible messages full of exclamation points suited him just fine. And although he avoided looking over his shoulder, he thought back to the blue and green three-dimensional images of what would occupy these sites in the future and imagined them sprayed over with jagged black lines, and for a long second had a vision of the spraying turning into someone's running amok. On one side the paintings, conciliatory. On the other side the graffiti: 'Unreconciled.' And at the same time he saw them as letters written between waking and sleeping, as mirror-writing, indecipherable.

It had been quite some time since he had made his way into the heart of the city, and how much had changed there! A new mayor had not only had the stones of the ancient rampart dug out but also the main river's tributaries, which in the previous century or two had been walled in and channelled underground; and some of these tributaries, fairly broad brooks with little water in them, could be crossed not only by way of bridges or overpasses but also, if one was on foot, by fords, using the blocks of stone laid on either side. Along the main river the logos of the previous mayor had been removed, along with the palm trees in wooden planters placed there during the summer and the sand dunes, brought in from who knows where, and the river had gone back to meandering, as it had from time immemorial in these latitudes, from east to west. Likewise, at one point, where the next two bridges connecting the left and right banks were the farthest apart of any in the entire city, the planned extra bridge had not been built. Instead a pedestrian ferry had been added, which, however, did not correspond to any tradition: no ferry had ever traversed the river at this point. The newly uncovered fords and the ferry, of a sort never built anywhere else: the actor, heading straight into town, boarded it, took it, remembering a film in which Spencer Tracy played a mayor of whom it was said, 'Let the world be governed not by statesmen but by mayors!'

It seemed to him then as if it were already 'terribly late'. The sun was still shining, however, though now with yet another quality of light, no sign of dusk; it was mid-summer, after all, even if a single withered leaf from a plane tree made a pre-autumnal hissing as it scooted along the pavement. So when he reached the opposite bank, where the inner districts continued, he took the steps down to the underground. For a while he rode back and forth. In the Metro, as on all public transportation in the city, by the bye, a regulation promulgated by the new mayor was in effect, according to which anyone who wanted to conduct a—what did it use to be called?—telephone call had to put on a special helmet that made the person using the telephone inaudible, the justification being that speaking on the telephone disrupted the general order and domestic tranquillity as much as relieving oneself in public. And thus he encountered another phenomenon that was new since his last hike through the centre years earlier: passengers either sitting in silence, their faces distorted inside their helmets made of Plexiglas or whatever, or, in the minority, those without helmets or headphones.

None of the latter were speaking. On his last trip through the inner city, many of the passengers had still been reading, books, mostly fat ones, which they were often far into, as if they had been riding the underground for a long time, completely preoccupied with their ceaseless spelling-out— their lips moved constantly—deciphering and reading. This time he saw only one person holding a book, and he was sitting in the rear on one of the fold-down seats, where the light was so dim that one had to be driven by tremendous yearning or curiosity to immerse oneself in a book. What might that person be reading, sitting in semi-darkness, as if sequestered from the others? He was an overweight man who could have used at least one more fold-down seat, and he had opened the book with a tenderness that seemed a mixture of timidity and reverence. My actor was dying with curiosity to see the author's name and the title, and he worked his way towards the reader, doing his best to remain inconspicuous. He would not have had to get that close, for the lettering on the book jacket jumped out at one even from a distance, that was how large it was, and phosphorescent to boot, like a neon sign. What was the book's title, and who was the author? Suffice it to mention that on a flight from Amsterdam to Edinburgh, let's say, every second passenger in the fully booked plane had had this same volume on his lap, with the same neon script on the cover.

Mounted on the wall above the reader was one of the small, framed advertising plaques one usually saw in the Metro, in black and white. It advertised evening classes and showed a teacher correcting papers, with a text indicating that he, the teacher, would not forgive himself if, despite being exhausted by the end of the day, he did not provide the help his student would need and instead switched on the television. An advertising text that, together with the gentle, serious countenance of the 'teacher'—a countenance on a commercial poster!—moved the actor, and when his eyes swept through the car, the passengers' faces, including the faces of those on their telephones, especially those merely pretending to be on the telephone, seemed saturated with a sadness that could not possibly become more intense. That did not merely seem so; it was so. In other respects they all remained impenetrable, revealing nothing, absolutely nothing, about themselves—their earlier lives, their stories, their why and wherefore. All there was to sense was something like a homicidal impulse, a desire to wage war. No, not to sense: to unlock, to sniff out, to smell. The car reeked of violence, a truly pestilential stench. At any moment one of them would pull a knife or something and attack the others. He had already spotted the one, standing there quietly, ramrod straight, recognizable by his fixed stare and even more distinctly by his taut cheeks. And as he let the man merge with him, he realized that this man was himself, his reflection in the car's black windows. Surprising, actually, that so few ran amok. And what if—the thought came to him suddenly—one who ran amok was at the same time sacrificing himself, wanting to save someone or something? Would the story, the film, be able to portray that? And the faces in the underground seemed strangely pacified by such a fantasy. One saw them differently. Every face became that of a star, especially those with closed eyelids: over there: Anna Magnani. And that one: Montgomery Clift. All the great films from the distant past returned in these faces, on these eyelid screens.

He took off his hat, and it seemed to him that in the course of this one day his hair had grown excessively long, as had—he bent his head—his fingernails. Hadn't his head-bending had the same effect up to now that touching the ground with his feet had had for that figure in Greek mythology, allowing him to recover his strength, the strength of a giant, in moments of surrender? (The name of that figure: gloriously forgotten.) He promptly raised his head, and his gaze scanned the car and the narrow glass doors at one end that led into the next car, where the few passengers visible appeared reduced in size and as if far away, looking in the dimmed light like emigrants bedded down in a ship, in a cabin on one of the lowest decks, with the passengers in the car beyond, the third one, merely a sensed presence, poor souls from limbo, the antechamber to hell, no longer in existence— its dimness brightened, however, by a Marilyn Monroe–blond male—while in the much brighter light of his own car a young woman next to him was reapplying her eyeliner, and the equally young woman beside her was putting on lipstick with similar care. They were rocking their heads to a music that did not come from plugs in their ears, unlike that of their fellow passengers. Two virgins, self-possessed—and how! Yes, did that still exist? It did. Next to him in a carrier a newborn, who looked up at him with the unspoken question: 'Father, why have you abandoned me?'

He emerged from the underground into daylight to find himself by one of the city's numerous squares, each of which considered itself a main square. According to daylight saving time—he continued to go by standard time, always subtracting an hour—it was evening by now, yet it was still light, if no longer so bright, because the sun, although it had not set (when would it finally set?), was covered by cumulus clouds, massing to the west high and higher and dark and darker. During the interlude in the Metro, the sky's blue had been extinguished; a bit of blue could be sensed more than seen in the east, and then it withdrew beyond the horizon, gone indefinitely.

A round plaza, appropriately so for a main square (or perhaps not). Thousands of cars, bumper to bumper and side by side, circulated around him, and it was as if the countless pedestrians around the rim of the plaza were also going in circles. In the middle of the plaza a giant screen had been set up, large enough for a stadium. On the screen a steady stream of images, both advertising and world news. Circling the plaza himself on foot, and then again, and then a third time, as if that were an indispensable part of his proceeding full-speed ahead. The screen meanwhile duplicated in all directions, without sound, or the sound inaudible in the evening traffic.

Again and again in the news broadcast a close-up of the president, with only a suggestion of his shoulders showing, in a dark suit, and a wall of bookshelves behind him as he delivered a solemn speech to the country. The actor had learnt to read lips, and thus he could decipher the speech being made by the president, in whose presence he in fact should have been at that very moment. At issue was a declaration of war, not described as such, however, but as a 'surgical strike', an 'intervention', 'retaliation', a 'response'. Citizens of this country, the lip-reader gathered, had been killed in another country, with the knowledge and, no doubt, involvement of those in power there, and that, by God, Creator of the Universe, could not be tolerated. And in closing the president spoke these words: 'We have no choice but to take up arms against the enemies of our civilization and our religion. This very night the operation will be launched, lest our history books record one day that our fellow countrymen gave their lives in vain. No, I give you my sacred word that our citizens shall not have died in vain! History demands justice and must take its God-given course. May God stand by us! Our God is great. All praise to Almighty God . . . '

That last part he intoned. The camera pulled back; the president rose from his seat in the library to his full height and left the room where the intervention had been announced. Striding, arms stretched away from his body but barely swinging, the gait of an experienced statesman, and not only in the performance of acts of state. Jogging in the morning, then striding, striding through the day, through the night. The hint of an involuntary mimicking by the actor of that striding as he circled the plaza. Breaking it off. Coming to a standstill? Pausing? Impossible. Onward, around and around the plaza. Walking resolutely was something else again. To regain that gait, he would have had to go considerably more slowly than his fellow pedestrians. Just as one could have strength to speed up, one could have strength to slow down. But that he no longer possessed in the present hour, and accordingly he moved at the pace of those around him, rolling his shoulders and taking steps that mimed energetic activity and that he, thinking of the president, and not only of him, called 'active walking'. Someone out of sight in the crowd suddenly cried out, his cry directed towards the image loop showing the president: 'Don't you idiots see—he has no face? And no power either? There is no power any more, only abuse. And that man abuses power! It's embarrassing to be alive. It's embarrassing to be that man's contemporary.' And another voice from someone out of sight: 'Right, are the rest of us on earth just trash?' And then a third person, also out of sight: 'Who came up with that statesman's stride, the most hypocritical stride there is, the stride of history-falsifiers?'

It was striking how often people trying to avoid each other in the crowd turned in the wrong direction and more or less collided, and how many cut each other off. And even more striking that, as he circled and circled, time and again he recognized someone, or thought he did. This had often happened to him in the centres of the world's great cities, and it always involved people from elsewhere, from somewhere else entirely, and from earlier, much earlier, from another life, often the deceased. But that evening he encountered people from that same day, from that morning, from the forest, from the outskirts and the in-between districts. The jealous man who had invaded the woman's property walked by with his arm hooked contentedly in that of a different woman. The forest dweller, only hours earlier not even able to crawl on all fours, sashayed around the plaza in an ankle-length silk coat, with a poodle on a leash and stinking, if at all, of the perfume currently in vogue in the capital, or was it the poodle that exuded the scent? The neighbours who had gone at each other in their gardens with axes, spears and World War bayonets marched past as a group, as numerous as it was harmonious, a couple of them with their arms around others, and one of them, the worst of the screamers, had turned into a woman, swaying her hips and batting her eyes as she pranced by on stiletto heels.

The only one from long ago whose path the actor crossed was his father. He recognized him, who knows why, by his white hair, although he was not the only white-haired person in the early-evening crowd. And he also did not come face-to-face with his father, saw only his white locks, and that for but a moment, followed, however, by one of the long seconds. He looked rakish out there, the old man, walking maybe several degrees faster than the others. He was headed to a dance in the ballroom of a hotel that had once been a Grand Hotel. In his light-coloured summer suit and his pointed tango shoes of soft leather with suede inserts, his father no longer looked like someone who had worked all his life with his hands. He had been to a hair salon, where he had combed his hair with a dab of gel in front of the largest mirror, and after that had received a mani- and pedicure from the Filipino girl who, when he tucked a banknote into her cleavage as usual, did not stop him, good Christian that she was. In the ballroom, he would dance with each of the older ladies—fewer and fewer of them each month—first the tango, then, when they were all tired, the waltz, one waltz after another as a finale, a finale that lasted longer with each month that passed. And before midnight, he would make his way home beyond the periphery to his little single-family house, where he lived alone with his canary, would sit in his vest, listening to the late news on the radio. Upon receiving word of his death, the son had pictured his father as someone who had done nothing but work all his life, although God knows that picture did not fit the facts. Curious, too, that he saw his own people in complete strangers, especially in the crowd, while his own people, whenever he had been in their presence, had seemed like complete strangers to him—he sometimes recognized them only after taking another look, or even the closest of looks. Hallo, Father, you old ladykiller!

On the giant screen, alternating with the constantly replayed declaration of war—or whatever it was—bodies and faces in advertisements were projected that seemed to be calibrated to the lines of cars and the thousands of people circling the plaza. A contrast, however, that caught one's attention: the contrast between the naked women, larger than life, in the advertisements up on the screen and the many veiled women below in the crowd. 'Not to see the other person's face, no gleam of eyes and likewise no gleam of hair, to be denied that gleam: can that be God's will? No, that is not God's will, for what gives one a premonition of Paradise is the beauty of women, together with the brightness of eyes in prayer! And it is equally contrary to God's will to project these naked women, whose faces, mouths, eyes and postures, not content to simulate Paradise, actually falsify the dream of Paradise, offending against and making it despicable. Ah, the longing for a countenance, equally removed from the veiled ones here and the false promises there, and also not seen only in black and white on a small placard in the underground—in colour, now, here on the square! The other person's face as medicine!'

Yet no matter how hard he looked, he did not see one. (Or did that have to do with how he went about it?) The women among the pedestrians on the large plaza were merely playing at being beautiful, and for him that was the opposite of the kind of play that would make the crucial difference. They were playing a game that was not their own.

Their seriousness, too, was a mask. And even from those who enjoyed playing their masked game a kind of helplessness communicated itself to him. Altogether, the feature common to those in the crowd, of the men as well as the women, was helplessness. Their lips were swollen with helplessness, and he imagined swollen lips like these behind the veils as well.

He looked up into the sky, still bright above the round plaza in spite of the sun's disappearance, while along the horizons the blackness of gathering thunderclouds was intensifying. The evening wind anticipated the storm to come with powerful gusts, and from high in the sky, as if from the parks and avenues of the entire city, swirled swarms of linden blossoms, with little balls on the stems, spinning as they fell and resembling, as they further dimmed the sky, a series of miniature parachute squadrons landing on the plaza. In that sky, empty and bright after the gusts subsided, streaks of clouds still bright as day, shot through with vapour trails, formed an X-ray image above the plaza that stretched across the entire firmament, ribs at right angles to each other, as if the entire skeleton were broken and fragmented, the X-ray revealing a being never before seen. This sky did not belong to the earth below or vice versa. And with it the thought that he would never return to his country, to his house and garden there.

The streetlights flickered on around the circle. No sky to be seen now, or even sensed. The actor peeled himself out of the crowd, found a table in one of the spacious eateries around the plaza, with a view of the scene outside through the large front windows, and there wrote a letter to his son, which went something like this: 'My dear son, as long as you were a child and an adolescent, I would have dropped everything for you—my profession, every woman, every pleasure. In you I saw someone who needed me as no one else did, even if you were not conscious of it. I saw you as a poor little creature and myself as your saviour. Then you became an adult, and I forgot about you. At first that upset me greatly, but as time passed it seemed to me that this phenomenon was universal. Is it universal? That a man's family consists not of his grown children but of his forebears, the dead? The only thing I ever wanted to be for you was the one who nurtured you. And the only thing I ever expected of you: that I might learn from you. And fundamentally that is how it still is. And so I await your judgement on me as your father.'

Not until he had stuck the letter into an envelope, among the possessions he still had on him, did it occur to him that for a long time now his son had had no address, making his way as he was across the continents, and, at the moment, following the example of his mother, the adventurer, and in her footsteps—which did not exist, since she had never left any traces—following the Yukon downstream in Alaska, looking, listening, recording sights (almost microscopic ones, at his feet) and sounds (those at the limits of audibility). How about sending him the letter electronically? The letter was a letter, and as such had to cover a distance in space and especially in time. It could not be in Alaska instantaneously; it had to travel, days and days. Only in that way would it arrive, and only in that way would the words he had written have an effect.

A letter box in classic yellow, as tall as a man, with two slots, one for local mail, the other for all points of the compass, stood outside on the pavement, within easy reach. From his seat by the window, open to the summer air, he could have thrust his letter through the open window into the 'all points' slot. But he just sat there and observed the letter box, as well as the activity around it. As night closed in, the number of people posting letters increased. Then came a period during which they streamed to the box from all sides, one after the other, finally clustering around the box, forming a queue, especially in front of the slot for long-distance and foreign post. Letters to official agencies and so on, with pre-printed addresses, were in the minority; most of the envelopes displayed handwriting. So after an era in which letter- writing had dried up. seemingly for good, letters were being written again. Can you believe it? The crowd grew larger and larger. 'End of days?' The footpaths alone, more and more of them, even in the heart of the capital, had belied that notion.

Human countenance, where art thou hiding? As he peered over his shoulder, it revealed itself, as if summoned by the question, at one of the tables in the back of the brightly lit eatery. Two young women were sitting there. Only one of them showed him her face. It was pale, but not with the pallor that comes of spending time in closed rooms. This pallor seemed to come above all from talking. And the woman talked and talked. But the way she talked! Without a single gesture, without any dramatic changes in expression, yet accompanying her words with subtle variations in her expression that added something to her face, that lit it from within and transformed it into a human countenance. As the woman talked, she expressed herself with all her soul, meanwhile remaining perfectly calm, without any suggestion of putting on a show. What was she saying? His lip-reading failed him in this case. What conveyed itself to him was simply astonishment, and at the same time a lament, commiseration (of a childlike sort), and at the same time gratitude, amusement, bemusement, all at once, accompanied by a constant nodding and head-shaking. She talked and talked, yes. What talk, however, utterly non-judgemental! Telling a story, yes, but there was something else as well. The way the woman talked, she was conjuring something up, something from the past and, at the same time, conjuring up something in the future, and above all and ultimately that was what gave her a human countenance. What a gift. There was nothing more. One needed nothing more.

Then, suddenly, the woman fell silent, in mid-sentence, and the actor saw from a distance that she was blushing—and how!

In that instant he recognized her. He recognized her from witnessing her blushing. She was the one, the woman with whom he had spent the night. Can you believe it! Time and again in his life he had mistaken those closest to him, members of his family, his child, for strangers when he saw them outside the house, in a public place, on the street, in the streetcar. He was filled with shame. But not because he had failed to recognize her, no, it was because he had just realized that she was speaking of him and herself, telling the other woman about herself and him, and it was this telling that made her face glow. Shame also overcame him because he recalled how that morning, alone in her house, he had decided to interrogate her when they returned in the evening. Ah, the irresponsibility that came of being alone. This was irreparable. He was not worthy of the woman. He did not deserve to be close to this human countenance. All the ravens of Alaska should fall upon him then and there! He had abused her love. He had betrayed her love. And he recognized how often he had been guilty of betrayal, or almost. Did that make him 'a typical actor', like the clueless ones, the stupidest of the stupid? The two of them, he and the woman there, had never had a real relationship. There had been nothing, nothing at all between them, until now. They had not even kissed, let alone nuzzled, let alone held each other. And now he deciphered retroactively what she had said: 'With him a door opens inside me that I did not know was there. And in love I have no expectations, for the first time—am only perplexed. Without meaning to, he saves me, and saves me again, and saves me yet again.' And what had he read in her face? That it, this face, was power, the true and proper power—and any abuse unthinkable.

As luck would have it, at that very moment the director in whose film he was supposed to perform the next day entered the eatery. The last person he wanted to see. Almost as bad as if he had run into a 'colleague' on the street. Nothing for it but to look away, get to his feet, and slip into the dining areas farthest to the rear! And as luck would have it again, there was an emergency exit back there, and in no time my actor had escaped into the open.

It fit the situation that there, only a short distance from the central plaza, he had to take but one step outside, although deep in the heart of the city, to find himself in an entirely different part of the world. Different sounds, different smells, a different air and light. Light? The area had no streetlights, and it was also not a street but a trail, a broad one, almost another square, seemingly left over from a much earlier time and overgrown with grass, bushes and saplings, the vegetation more wild if possible than in the clearing up on the plateau beyond the outskirts. How could he see all that without streetlights, without lights in houses?

He saw it, and besides, in the sky all around there was a constant flickering of heat lightning, without thunder, in whose flashes the details appeared sharply, more sharply than in any other light, and the darkness that followed left an after-image of a caved-in wooden fence, of tumbledown cottages—reminding him of the land of the ancient river—of a rusted-out cement mixer.

For a long time he stood there motionless, in the heart of the city and at the same time transported into something for which an archaic word came to him: a demesne. The nocturnal roaring, screeching, and shoving around the plaza behind him continued unabated, but here in the demesne it seemed more like a radio drama, consisting entirely of sound effects, and also turned down low, just a faint backdrop of sound. The most prominent noise was the rustling of bushes and the rattling of the other wild vegetation in the night wind, and that although the wind, as usual in the presence of heat lightning, was quite gentle—when it did not subside altogether—coming closer in the demesne 'by a whole world'—yet another expression that occurred to him—and intervening more profoundly than in any other natural setting devoid of human beings. Yes, by a whole world, and as the whole world, with the windless moments wafting with nothing but whooshing of air. And in-between, a ceaseless grating sound, as if from within the earth, the chorus of crickets, and it, too, unlike in the middle of the woods beyond, not other-worldly, or at least closer to the world than the noise backdrop of the central plaza.

He would not have been surprised if another falcon's feather had fallen at this very moment from the heat-lightning-filled sky, the third one, or even a feather from the summer eagle. He looked up involuntarily but saw only evening and night flights following one another in quick succession, their wing-tip lights blinking. Too late for a falcon's screech, and much too late for an eagle's bleating. At most an owl hooted.

The next flare of heat lightning lit up, for a second's duration, a cloud directly overhead against the black sky that had the shape of an hourglass, and it felt as if it were indicating the approaching end of summer. Time to return from the demesne to 'the sectors'.

But first, as he made his way through the dark-ness, someone addressed him, using the title of one of his films. A good-evening greeting preceded it. 'Good evening, Sir, Gospodine, Mister, Señor, Sahib "Ford-Crosser"!' For the first time this day, the actor had been recognized. How could that be, in the dark? Or had a flash of heat lightning shown the other person his profile? That must have been it: he had been recognized by his profile, plucked out of the darkness, and in contrast to everything else that had happened to him, for a change he did not object to being recognized this way. He found this kind of recognition refreshing. Besides, the voice of the invisible person greeting him—the actor did not turn to look the next time the heat lightning flared—had been amiable, a voice expressing no surprise at coming upon the star at such a time and in such a place. It was natural to come upon him in this demesne; it was appropriate for his profession. And the other man: What was he doing there? Nothing special. He was sitting in the dark on a discarded upside-down fruit crate amid the silent heat lightning, supposed never to end but to go on and on, sitting there and letting the heat lightning flash, as silent as the heat lightning itself. And in the demesne a letter box turned up, seemingly just installed, and he deposited the letter to his son in it. The letter would reach its destination, of that he was certain, and soon.

NINE

Up to the hour of the night when it had been arranged that he would pick up the woman from her workplace, the actor roamed from one centre to the next, crossing the river, then using the next bridge or the one after that, to cross back, and so on. It was as if from now on he must not stop, let alone come to rest anywhere. It was crucial that he not get drawn in by anything, and not allow anyone to block his way. The important thing was to arrive in one piece and give any possible danger a wide berth. Something was at stake. Much was at stake. Everything. And no one must know that he was carrying a diamond in his breast pocket, in comparison to which the famous one—what was it called?—was a mere bauble; that, furthermore, he was on a secret mission.

The second thunderstorm, the evening storm he had wished for, to follow the morning one, failed to materialize. The heat lightning had ceased. The warm night brought more people out into the streets and squares, onto the bridges. (An involuntary image of clouds of frosty breath.) Only in the buses did the number of passengers gradually dwindle, and although during the day the majority of them had scrambled up to the upper deck, the few nocturnal passengers all stayed below. Seeing one face, that of the woman, had been enough for him now to see more and more of them, and that was no illusion such as occurs when one has seen a snake and afterwards sees snakes squirming wherever one looks. Perhaps he, the actor, was doing his part to give the people in the crowd faces, was responsible for their acquiring faces. Now he was following the woman's path, one of the routes she took every day, and intentionally so. And for the space of a second the thought flashed through him that retracing the other person's path had once been considered part of 'love's labour'.

At the same time he remained on guard. Murderers and perpetrators of violence were out and about, unrecognized. But he recognized them, and knew they must not be allowed to sense that he recognized them. Otherwise they would attack him instantly. One, realizing that his cover had been blown, stuck out a leg to trip him up, and a woman wheeled around and struck him in the back, screaming: Why was he looking at her that way?—the only sentence audible on this stretch— and took to her heels. He could not take any more chances. Not usually a dancer, he now practised the avoidance dance. And one time he did take a chance after all, intentionally heading towards one such killer, who promptly jumped to one side and ducked, like a cat. In a film, a close-up would have showed his terrified face. Here in reality the killer stammered something like an apology.

In his imagination, he was on the verge of reaching his goal, after a difficult journey. With the goal in sight it was tempting to relax one's guard, and then it could happen. Could happen how? In the sense that a young mother who was crossing the street at an intersection simply walked away from her child, who had been bawling the entire time because he would not, or could not, go a step farther, left him standing there bawling, lit a cigarette, and without turning her head to look at him continued on her way, and the child now howled, the way billions of children had howled since the night of time, and yet it was for the first time on this particular night, and then came the thought: 'There, it's happening.'

He must not let it happen to him, so he looked down at the pavement, at the tar and cobblestones, and whenever he sensed danger he took evasive action, doubling back, contrary to his usual practice. His back and forth across the river was not a stroll. Once, when frantic barking and growling made itself heard on a quiet street and suddenly a pack of dogs, one hundred strong and seemingly with a thousand tails, burst around the corner and shot towards him, he remained calm, remembering the myth of the ancient Greek actor and singer (the name? 'I've forgotten') who was torn apart by such a pack, and told himself he would not have been able to play that role, either on the stage or in a film, and even these wild dogs would sense this and rush past him—as they then did. One of the dogs even trotted along beside him for a while, as if taking him for his long-lost master.

He would have wished for less light as he approached his destination. But this was a city of light, and even in the side streets there was so much brightness that, he thought, 'there was no escaping'. It was as bright as day, and yet entirely different, with pitch darkness not high in the sky but halfway up. He remembered the tale of the country bumpkins who think they can catch the daylight in buckets or scoops and carry it into windowless houses, and imagined an opposite situation in which darkness might be scooped into excessive brightness.

Amid this brightness he ran into a dying man who, all lit up, like the people standing around him, was lying on the tiled floor of a Metro entrance. Although the actor did not stop anywhere, it was an encounter. Their eyes met. The dying man looked at him as if he had been waiting for him. How the actor knew that he was dying? He knew—such things he still knew. And he also knew that the man was not looking to him for help. These motionless but not yet broken eyes had expressed: I recognize you! You've been recognized! And they continued to say that after he had continued on his way, and would say that till the hour of his own death. The actor had been recognized by the dying man not as the person who . . . as had happened earlier in the demesne. But? 'He recognized me, that was all.' And then he added, talking to himself, 'Those eyes meant well by me. They mean well. They will have meant well. But what if it is already too late?' And out in the street, in the midst of the crowd, he crossed himself and, as he did so, he recalled that he had crossed himself this way once before, with a similar sweeping gesture. Where? Not in a church. But? Before entering a child's room. And now he was grateful for the brightness in the city of light, where every corner was brightly lit, where rays of light streamed from the empty and ever emptier buses driving by into the eye sockets of the dying man. He forgot the danger. No more doubling back. From now on, straight ahead, in the night wind. 'Hallo there, Captain Night Wind!' he said, almost singing.

By the front door of a house in the middle of the city, tiny in comparison to those next door, balloons for a child's birthday party, and from inside laughter, not weary at all despite the lateness of the hour, with a rising cadence that made one think of a lark, not the way it sang but the way it rose in the air, higher and higher into the sky.

By contrast the laughter in the street: one wanted to share in the pleasure, but what was it? One did not understand this laughter breaking out here and there in the crowd, one could not picture anything that might cause it, and it was not contagious. How contagious laughter had been in childhood, especially when it came from the stage, for instance, from a magic play. Yet it was his fundamental seriousness that had destined him for the actor's profession. Serious through and through, he longed for laughter.

It was striking how much sighing made itself heard among the passers-by, almost all of them young, out of which his rapid walking fashioned a kind of sigh chorus, not unlike that of the elderly folk on the outskirts. Added to it another sentence that could be made out clearly, a single one: 'You have no compassion.' The multitude of wheeled suitcases being pulled in every direction likewise began to speak whenever they rolled from smooth pavement onto a stretch of cobblestones. What did they say? In the asphalt of the avenues and boulevards, tank tracks, from the last war? From the parade on the national holiday? Bellowing from not that far away, seeming to come closer, sounding like people being led to the slaughter, no, coming from a football stadium, and the shrill sound in-between was the referee's whistle. An open church door, and in the interior, filled to the last seat and if possible even brighter than the floodlit squares, a late-evening Mass taking place, the Lord's Prayer at that moment, in a never-heard alternative version: 'And deliver us from ourselves, the evil!' Or had he misheard? No, that was no Mass. It was just many people, many, many, a crowd, the crowd that had come together for prayer, a tempestuous prayer, shouted out more and more as if with one voice, the bodies of the worshippers squeezed in side by side: not a gap into which the evil spirits from outside could slip! Desperate praying? No, this shouted prayer was not desperate. There was no such thing as desperate praying.

In a park or square—there, too, no spot that was not bright as day—two boys, or children, one bigger, the other smaller, on a swing, one boy sitting on the other's knees, facing him, and the two pairs of legs extending in opposite directions, another letter, not yet seen, new to the alphabet.

Many people who were lost, to whom he, the stranger there, gave directions in passing. Sending them astray? What if he did? How often his father had lost his way, which the son had always realised immediately but had followed his lead nonetheless.

A shop window with nothing in it but apples, made if possible even brighter by the night, or bright in a different way. At a traffic light the beauty and the beast, she over here, he over there, then meeting in the middle of the street when the light turned green and becoming a couple. Another beautiful woman passed by, and all the weary people sitting on *café* terraces or at bus stops paused in mid-yawn, and the only one who continued yawning was a blind man. Someone, an adult, a child, was writing with a finger in the night air. Someone, a child, a woman, an old man, hopped. Did someone in the crowd seek someone else's eyes? On all the escalators people stopped walking as soon as they got on, including those who had just been running, and let themselves be carried. Time and again people running, several together, too many, and not for athletic purposes. Fireworks and more fireworks—fireworks? Really? Were these people condemned to war until the end of time? Nowhere looks expressing such open hostility as those that parents directed towards their children. And vice versa? No. By avoiding his love for the woman up to now, he had preserved their serenity. Or not? What language was it in which one added an aspirated sound to the word for 'pain' and it became the word for 'world'? Don't know. Do know something else, though. And this other knowledge is power—power.

And now the squirrel in Nome, Alaska, the squirrel on boulders by the Bering Sea, facing towards Russia. What elicited these images from distant times and places? Don't know, don't want to know. What was clear: these places, things and beings turning up unexpectedly and silently were sights, sights appropriate to the current time, sights deserving of the name. Were they the last ones still possible for a person of today? A few measures of street music, short blasts on trumpets, and a clarinet that wove its sound around the trumpets and drowned them out, played by people who would never go home again, and had never been at home anywhere, a flourish of triumphal sorrow. 'I'm with you. Grab me by the scruff of my neck and transport me away from here!' A few measures of music were enough to bring one to a halt. To grab oneself by the scruff of the neck and head for another planet? No, this is our planet.

What a day. What a night. He wanted to say that out loud, wanted to shout it—it would have been his first shout—but he could not get out a single word. Had he lost his voice? How would he speak his part the next day? On the other hand, the man in the script who ran amok was almost mute. If he had seen someone like the passer-by here rubbing his eye with his finger, without a word he would have poked that same finger into that same eye. The hero of the book he had read that morning, brought close to running amok by his rage at the malice of the object—that one lemon seed that kept slipping away from him—has become reconciled, however, to objects by the time evening comes—has no more resentment of them—and even makes a speech thanking them: 'Thank you, apple seeds, for letting yourselves be picked up from the ground so easily. Thank you, pencil lead, for breaking only once today. Thank you, shoelaces, for coming undone only twice . . . '

He felt an urge to bring the woman a gift. No, he was no gift-giver. He just wanted to give something, this very moment. A chair on the sidewalk, a single one, discarded, caught his eye in the night wind, and he picked it up and carried it with him for a stretch. In the next street he gathered up pieces of paper that the wind was blowing around —parking passes, cash-register receipts, shopping lists, movie tickets (for films shown the previous month, long since forgotten). In earlier days he would have found something to read among all those slips of paper, something to study, to take along. A couple with their arms around each other passed, and again words became audible, when the man said to the woman, 'My apple!'

One time, during his days on the stage, the actor had got stuck saying his lines and, although he did not freeze, he simply stood there motionless, his head bowed, until the curtain closed. Just so a man, a very young one, now stepped out of a house onto the pavement. He remained standing by the door and a bunch of keys fell from his hand. He not only let the keys lie there; he also lost his grip on his briefcase, or computer, or whatever it was, and it crashed to the ground, likewise a mobile telephone, or was it an eyeglass case? The young man made no effort to bend down for these objects, but also did not go on his way, just stood there on the nocturnal pavement. As the actor watched, his own telephone, or whatever he had in his hand at that moment, almost slipped out of his grasp, and the other man's paralysis communicated itself to him. Then he pulled himself together, stepped off his path—which was allowed in this situation—gathered up the things scattered on the sidewalk, and pressed them, sternly, one after the other, into the young man's arms and to his chest. He, the actor, now embodied power, was the local elder. His work done, he gave the stranger a hug, and the man, without a word, as if his saviour did not exist, went briskly on his way.

After that a woman on a bench, she, too, very young, and her lover had just left her, and she knew it was for good. Being abandoned would haunt her to the end of days. There would never be anyone else for her. And besides she had lost her job on this day, and all her savings before that. She was done for, once and for all. She was weeping. Or was she laughing, silently, with her entire face? Strange: as some people wept for joy, others laughed in pain? Misery. A universe of pain. He could not go to this stranger and take her, too, in his arms, could he? Yes, embrace them all, as No-man. He had always been most effective when he became No-man, the actor, effective less as a man of action than as an avoider, he, of all people, the man who had once worked with his hands. How proud he had once been of his professions, both of them! Embrace her? But she could no longer be helped, right? And, as so often before, he was close to collapsing under the weight of others' misery. But now the fact that she could not be helped filled him instead with wild rage, against her, the lost soul. To hurl himself at her and stab her with a knife as he had done to the president that morning, 'unfortunately only in my thoughts'.

And he came within a hair's breadth of doing it.

As he walked he punched in the number of the one and only. How uplifting it was to do nothing but count, consciously deal with numbers. And how uplifting a person's voice could be, a rarity amid all the voices. She immediately greeted him by name, no need for him to open his mouth or even pop the telephone helmet over his head. Her night's work was done, and she was waiting for him on the square in front of one of the cathedrals in this former city of kings, in front of the Bar du Destin; the Bar de l'Espérance next door was not for them.

Then another giant screen without any sound, and the image just graphics, a computer game magnified to a thousand times its size, representing a kind of radar screen in the cockpit of a bomber, and in the middle of the screen, at intervals, the graphic representation of 'bomb' strikes, portrayed at a distance as a heart, boom, boom. Can you believe it, circling the plaza, which was also round, were buses, these, unlike the normal ones, darkened, some even completely black, also longer, more streamlined, and in addition—was this a joke?—suddenly many passers-by marching in double time, with blackened faces, while others— a film? a night shoot?—assumed a stride like models on a runway, and, between these two armies, solitary individuals, the homeless, dragging themselves along, hauling their housewares-without-a-house stuffed into dozens of plastic bags, on the way to their sleeping places under the stars as one-man caravans, knitted woollen caps on their heads at the height of summer. Black followed black, bundled-up figures followed bundled-up figures, with even their hands bundled up, masks followed masks, figures covered with tattoos followed figures covered with tattoos, even in the hollows of their knees. If my actor wept now, he would have to die of weeping. Why not, after all? The Alaska woman had commented one time that his entire being consisted of unwept tears. People were coming out of a cinema, the last show. Was one man crying? Some quickly wiped away their tears. In response to one who was also crying, only more tears. As he passed by, the actor struck his brow with his fist and wanted to bash his head against a wall, or blacken his face, though differently from the crowd.

Instead, he turned into a juggler, with two apples, tossing them way up into the darkness, and each time he caught them; not once did an apple slip from his hands. So he was still a good catcher, not only a thrower, a thrower and catcher in one, by night as by day, the quintessential catcher? He wished for a mythical creature—and here it was: a raven, his heraldic animal, up on a window ledge. Can you believe it! A raven in the middle of the night. But why did it not move, its talons curved motionless around the parapet, its head and beak likewise motionless? It was a dummy, installed to scare away the pigeons. But then a real raven appeared, swooping up from the ground into the night wind as only a raven could. 'If I need a haven, I'll call upon the raven'—that, too, he sang, almost.

Yes, this was the City of Good Paths, not only because of the hiking paths, the last stretch marked with a stone as large as a dolmen, left over from the network of royal roads, with a deeply incised crown, almost worn away, that of the royal miracle healer after whom the square in front of the cathedral was named. A glance at his hand as it traced the contours—the nails had grown unnaturally long in the course of this day, and a few fine reddish hairs had joined those already on his fingers.

The small square by the cathedral lit up like the rest of the city's centre. But the many protrusions and niches on the house of God created channels for shadows, and next to the building stood three trees so close together that they formed a forest, a dark forest in the heart of the megalopolis. Unlike the other squares in the centre, this one was unpaved; the reddish-yellowish soil on which the city was built, an airborne soil, lay there bare, slightly heaved, and where the sun had dried the morning's rain it displayed a pattern of five- and six-pointed shapes such as dried earth displays the world over. To pause there—permissible now— that, too, had an animating effect. Furthermore, after the blackness overhead, the sky finally became visible. Or had it been visible long since and he had simply not looked up? The moon gave the night a shimmer, and it was a half-moon, and when my actor reached the square, it was aligned with the cross on the tower, surmounted by a gilded rooster. 'To experience another sunrise!' Why did this thought come to him? The moon reflected in the rain puddles, which also reflected a bat fluttering by. Was he mistaken, or was dew falling already, before midnight? Taking off his hat and letting one of the falcon feathers float across the square. His hair felt damp, and then his upturned palm as well. Below the moon, like a hot-air balloon's gondola, a single star—Venus or Mars? Don't know. It could not be Orion, or whatever it was called, for it was not winter, nor could it be the Pleiades, or whatever they were called.

In the tree, a deciduous tree, a bird was sleeping, its feathers puffed up, the foliage and the bird merging into one. In front of the bar of destiny many guests were still sitting. He recognized the woman from afar. Sitting there, she was a woman with a mission, though in contrast to his hers was obvious at first sight, and, as always, she made a point of not looking in his direction. She was thirsty. Not only she but also the rest of those sitting there appeared to him as the Saints of the Last Days, different from the usual guests. Hunger and thirst, thirst and hunger. His heart pounded like a bucking wild horse. 'So, solitary hunter.' Above the church portal, in block letters, the theme or whatever, the sermon for Sunday or whenever: WHY DO YOU SEEK THE LIVING AMONG THE DEAD? From far off, a voice echoing through the night, bellowing at intervals: 'Shut up! Ta gueule!' Or was it an echo? No: echoes, reverberations had been eliminated some time ago, as had the gusts of air after the passage of trains, buses and trucks. How lost they both were, how—dislocated, dislocated in body and soul, he here and she there, lost beneath the sky, to themselves and also to each other. To fall upon and fight each other, rend each other limb from limb until they drew blood, to the point of no return, for life and death. To wrestle with each other until heaven, or some third party, or whoever or whatever, took pity on them both and they were set right with each other for life, now and until the hour of their death.

Silence on the square, enlivened by soft voices. The houses in that quarter, with the exception of the cathedral, all small, ground-hugging, more like cottages, though all with a mansard roof en miniature. In one of the houses or cottages, clearly audible, footsteps, slow and ponderous: a mother going up the wooden staircase to the mansard and into the prodigal son's unoccupied room. Inconsolable humming. 'Grant that . . . ' Grant what?

He stood and stood and stood. A third hunger, the great one. Time for the second Gentle Run.

Instead—the Great Fall.

Great Falls, Montana
July–September 2011